MYSTERY DOCTOR

MYSTERY DOCTOR

Claire Vernon

Chivers Press • G.K. Hall & Co.
Bath, England Thorndike, Maine USA

This Large Print edition is published by Chivers Press, England, and by G.K. Hall & Co., USA.

Published in 2000 in the U.K. by arrangement with Robert Hale Ltd.

Published in 2000 in the U.S. by arrangement with Juliet Burton Literary Agency.

U.K. Hardcover   ISBN 0-7540-3937-4   (Chivers Large Print)
U.K. Softcover   ISBN 0-7540-3938-2   (Camden Large Print)
U.S. Softcover   ISBN 0-7838-8759-0   (Nightingale Series Edition)

The text of this Large Print edition is unabridged.
Other aspects of the book may vary from the original edition.

Set in 16 pt. New Times Roman.

Printed in Great Britain on acid-free paper.

British Library Cataloguing in Publication Data available

Library of Congress Cataloging-in-Publication Data

Vernon, Claire.
    Mystery doctor / by Claire Vernon.
        p.   cm.
    ISBN 0-7838-8759-0 (lg. print : sc : alk. paper)
    1. Large type books.   I. Title.
    [PR6072.E735M97   2000]
    823'.914—dc21   99–42645

CHAPTER ONE

Peter Richardson slammed the surgery door shut after the last patient had gone. A tall thin man, with a tired-looking lean face and pointed chin, he slumped in his chair and stared at the pile of paper-work waiting to be done.

The door quietly opened and Iris Long came in.

'Dr. Rugg would like to see you at once, Dr. Richardson. He says it's urgent.'

'Oh for crying out loud!' Peter Richardson growled, 'Can't I have a moment's peace?'

The pretty blonde girl hesitated, 'You're not feeling too good, Doctor?'

Peter jumped to his feet, pushing his chair back roughly so that it fell over. 'I am perfectly well, Miss Long, thank you. Perfectly well indeed . . .'

He stumbled slightly as he made his way to the door, slammed it behind him and walked up the stairs to his flat. He'd have a drink first. It had been a long and hard day and he only wanted to be left alone! What the hell could David want to see him for?

In his austerely neat flat, Peter had a stiff Scotch, then went down to the floor below and walked into his partner's study.

David Rugg, a short, plump man with a

1

lop-sided smile and worried eyes, looked up.

'Thanks Peter. Sit down.'

'I prefer to stand. What's the big idea? Sending for me like a headmaster about to thrash one of the boys?'

David laughed. 'You're so right, Peter, old man. That is precisely what I'm about to do. Look, it's no good trying to hide it. That's the third time you've blacked-out this week. I wondered why you wanted the chauffeur for it's not like you.'

Peter fidgeted a little, avoiding David's eyes. 'I thought I shouldn't risk driving.'

'Quite right too, old man.' David got up and walked round so that they were only a foot or two apart. 'Well, Peter, this is the show down. You're off tomorrow for six months leave.'

'I'm ...' Peter opened his mouth and gasped. 'I am most certainly not ...'

'You most certainly are ...' David said, 'I've got Glen Peakes to stand in for you. He and his wife are arriving tomorrow to have your flat.' He tossed a key on the desk, 'Amelia's cousin, Mrs. Trent, has a cottage on the Cornish coast. She says you can have it for six months.'

Suddenly feeling exhausted Peter sank into a chair, staring up at his partner, whose face was unusually stern.

'Look, David,' Peter said in a conciliatory tone. 'I've had a check-up. I know what's wrong. I just have to slow down. I don't need

2

to go to Cornwall to do that.'

'Yes, you do, old man. And we're having no arguments about it. I am the senior partner, if you remember. You're very valuable to me, Peter, but not as a sick man. I can spare you better for six months than to lose you altogether. Get me?'

'David, you can't be serious. What the hell would I do in a cottage on the Cornish coast for six months?'

David shrugged his broadish shoulders. 'Search me. That's your problem. Just forget everything and, a word of advice, don't let anyone know who you are. Once they know, they'll be asking questions, giving you their problems and whatever. I want you to forget this life completely—then you'll come back to it refreshed. Peter, old man, let's face it. This has been hovering for a long time. I can't remember when you took a holiday.'

Peter smiled ruefully, 'Neither can I, to be honest.'

'Exactly. Your work is your life, I know, but it does us all good to relax now and again. That's all, old man. By the way, Amelia says do come to dinner tonight for we won't be seeing you for six months.'

Peter stood up wearily, picked up the key and put it in his pocket. 'Thanks. Got the address?'

'Amelia has. She'll give it to you tonight. By the way, Peter . . .' David's voice changed, sounded wary, 'Are you involved with Lucille Harding?'

'Good Lord, no! What made you think that?'

David shrugged. 'Just some rumours going around. Started by her, I think. Better watch out, Peter. Stronger men than you have gone to their doom.'

Peter managed a laugh. 'Not this man. I'm anti-marriage. You ought to know that. I don't think men like us should marry.'

'Amelia is a wonderful woman.'

David beamed. 'I couldn't agree more. I know it's a tough life for wives, but, damn it all, they do know before they marry you.'

'Maybe they don't realize it sometimes. Anyhow, don't worry about me, David. I've no interest in Lucille.'

'That's not the point. She has plenty of interest in you. Going to let her know?'

'Know? Oh! I see. Heavens above, no. I don't want her down there, hanging around.'

'Good. See you later.'

'Yes.' Peter went very slowly up the stairs and to his flat. There were a lot of things he must do if he was to move out the next day. Hell, why had David to spring this on him? He smiled ruefully because knowing himself, he understood why. *Au fait accompli* those were David's words where Peter was concerned. Peter, David always said, was obstinate and impossible! Was he? Peter wondered, as he set to work to sort out clothes and his personal belongings.

Six months on the Cornish coast! And this was just March. Could anything be more ghastly? he wondered. What on earth was he going to do with himself? It was like solitary confinement!

He'd drive down, slowly. Two days on the journey for he could call in on the Nelsons for the night. They were always inviting him. He had to take things slowly. He had sense enough to recognize that, no matter what David's opinion of him was!

But six months of doing nothing! How would he survive?

CHAPTER TWO

Gillian was riding down the hill when she saw a car parked outside Puffin Cottage.

The 'cottages' were spaced at intervals, most of them having been converted into permanent residences but this one was still a holiday cottage. Gillian knew that the Trents, who owned it, usually lent it to relatives and friends but this time, Gillian knew, they had rented it to a stranger. She wondered what sort of person would choose to come to Cornwall on a cold, wet March day like this.

She saw the man was having difficulties in

5

opening the front door. As she slid off the big horse she called out:

'Having trouble?'

He swung round as if startled and for a moment, they gazed at one another. Gillian saw a tall man with a long thin unhappy face. The man saw a slip of a girl with short dark hair clinging wetly to her pointed face. Her eyes were slightly slanted and green, he noticed with surprise, for it was unusual with dark hair! She wore jodhpurs and a green sweater with a polo neck.

'The damned door won't open,' he said irritably, 'the key turns but . . .' he paused, annoyed when he saw she was smiling. He was tired, wet, cold and fed-up. He could see nothing funny in the situation. 'I think someone has bolted the door.'

'Of course—I should have known,' the girl said. 'Trust old Kitty. She comes into the cottage once a week to clean it and has a thing about burglars so always bolts the door. Just come round the back . . .'

She led the way round the squat, stone-walled cottage. There were only a few plants in the garden and they looked pretty miserable.

As if she read his thoughts, she glanced up at him. 'That's the pity when the cottage is used for holiday people only. No one bothers about the garden. Are you staying for long?'

Her eyes were frankly curious and he was tempted to say it was none of her business, but he had to admit to himself that it must seem very strange for a man of his age to come and bury himself in a miserable place like this, especially in March when it was cold and wet.

'Six months.'

He saw her eyebrows lift in amazement for a moment and then she smiled. 'Good. Then you'll be able to do something with the garden. It's an absolute eye-sore at the moment. Dad's mad about gardening, he'll give you plants and seeds. Why've you come here?'

Peter Richardson hesitated for he was not a good liar. Yet if he told her the truth, the reason for his six month's hibernation would be revealed and the whole point lost. What he needed was to be left in peace, and not to have a crowd of women fussing round him as they surely would. What could he say to make the locals leave him in peace?

'I'm writing a book,' he said, startled yet pleased by the sudden idea he'd had.

The girl clapped her hands like a child. She looked about fifteen but then, he thought, that might mean anything for girls these days of nearly forty looked young.

'How absolutely smashing. We've got an artist here already.' Gillian said eagerly. 'At least he comes down at week-ends. Now we'll have an author.'

The grey clouded sky seemed to open and the rain poured down. Peter glanced up impatiently and Gillian stood on tiptoe as she took the key down from under the roof.

'That's the back door key.'

He frowned as he unlocked the door. 'Your Kitty must be daft. I thought she was afraid of burglars.'

The girl followed him into the kitchen, 'Oh, she is. That's why she leaves the key there. You see, she thinks the modern burglar is too intelligent to look for it in such an obvious place.'

Peter was looking round him and his depression increased though the kitchen was spotless with bright yellow walls, the curtains in check material yellow and white. There was a calor gas stove. Electric light and no oil lamps, such as he had half feared. There was a small fridge, a dresser with blue and white china. And then he realized something.

'Good grief,' he said, furious with himself. 'I've no food! I should have stopped in the village and got some.'

'You've brought nothing?' Gillian said, her eyes widening. 'Honestly ...' she began to laugh. 'You men!'

She led the way into the front room. This was pleasant, also, but hardly the background to which he was accustomed, he thought dourly. Bright rose and blue cretonne covers for the two arm-chairs, also a table and three small chairs. A bright blue rug on a polished floor. Bright purple curtains, doubtless to match the front door that the girl was

8

unbolting. She moved quickly, bringing in his two suitcases, going to the small grate where a fire was laid and lighting it, carefully fanning the flame until it crackled as the dry wood caught fire. She moved so fast that she had done all that before he realized what she was doing.

She sat back on her heels and smiled at him. 'I guess you're like most men,' she said, 'horribly spoiled.'

He took off his wet mackintosh and gave a sheepish, lopsided grin. 'I guess I am. I'm ...' He stopped in time, remembering David's advice that he was not to tell the locals the truth. 'I had a flat in a friend's house and their servants looked after me,' he said and smiled again.

The girl shook her head. 'Poor you and now you're landed with this. I bet you don't even know how to boil an egg.'

Peter laughed and was startled as he realized it was the first time he'd laughed for three days!

'You're so right but I can learn.'

The girl jumped up with a quick, graceful movement, 'Afraid you'll have to. Old Kitty will come in and clean up if you like every day but she can't come and cook. She has an old Mum and an invalid son to look after. Tell you what, I'll teach you, if you like.'

'Thanks,' he said. 'Maybe we should introduce ourselves. I'm Peter Richardson.'

'I know,' she smiled at him. 'Mrs. Trent wrote to Old Kitty and she'd lost her specs and asked me to read the letter to say you were coming.'

Peter caught his breath. David had assured him . . .

' "Mr. Peter Richardson . . ." ' Gillian quoted, ' "will be coming to stay for an indefinite period and the cottage must be prepared, for he is used to the best", Mrs. Trent said.'

Peter felt himself relax. 'Well, you know who I am but I don't know who you are.'

The girl laughed. 'I'm Gillian Yelton. I live in the house at the bottom of the hill, just before the road divides. I have a riding school and in the summer, I do quite well . . .'

'But what on earth do you do in the winter?' Peter had relaxed in an armchair, feeling the welcome heat from the fire as it crackled cheerfully.

Gillian, perched on the arm of the other chair, smiled.

'Odd things. Anything that goes. Baby sitting, looking after old folk, helping people decorate. Just anything.'

Peter frowned. 'How old are you?'

'Twenty. Why?'

'I just wondered. You look about fifteen. Surely you must *do* something? I mean, you can't just do *nothing*.'

Gillian laughed. 'Believe me I don't do *nothing*. I'm always busy. There's plenty to do

10

here. Sometimes I wish the day was forty-eight hours long. I live with my parents and . . .'

He was puzzled. 'But you can't just drift through life. I mean, you're well-educated, obviously intelligent, young—the whole world is your oyster. You could do anything. You must have some ambition.'

Gillian gave an odd laugh. 'Sure, I have an ambition.'

'What is it? Why are you wasting these years?'

Her face was grave. 'I don't think I'm wasting them.' She spoke thoughtfully, not annoyed by his remark but obviously considering it. 'I'm learning all the time, gaining experience.'

'But . . .' Peter began and paused for he realized that now he was interfering and it was none of his business.

'Well, everything I learn can help me,' Gillian told him gravely. 'You see my ambition is to get married and have four children.'

He stared at her as if amazed. 'And you call that ambition?'

Gillian was laughing. 'Honestly, I would have thought you'd agree with me. You're so terribly square, Mr. Richardson. I thought you'd believe that a woman's place was in the home. Obviously you don't. Neither do I— unless you're made that way. I am. I want my own home, my own husband and my own babies. It's as simple as that. Now . . .' She

11

jumped up. 'I've a lot to do but you're looking pretty tired so just relax and I'll get things organized for you.'

He started to get up and then realized just how weary he was. 'It was a long journey. It's very good of you. You drive? You could borrow my car.'

Gillian smiled. 'Now that's the nicest compliment I've ever had. No, I've got to get Black Bessie home and I'll come back in my car. I'll bring you enough food for several days. Have you any hates?'

'Any hates?'

She smiled. 'Yes, hates. Mine are sausages and cheese.'

He had to smile. 'I adore *them*. My hates are spaghetti, rice and spinach.'

'Good. I shan't be very long but you'd better keep an eye on the fire. There's plenty of logs in that cupboard. It's going to be a cold night. See you . . .'

Before he could move, she had gone out of the front door and he heard her calling her horse, grazing on the grass. He stood up very slowly, made up the fire and then went to the kitchen, found a glass, filled it with cold water and swallowed his tablets.

He went into the bedroom. A large double bed. Carefully made with a red coverlet to match the curtains. A big old-fashioned wardrobe that dominated the room. A small bathroom leading out of it. On the other side,

12

was another bedroom with two beds in it this time. He wondered why old Kitty had made up the double bed, had she concluded he would be coming with his wife? He sighed. He was too tired to bother to change the sheets and blankets and went back to the arm-chair and the warm fire.

How quiet it was. How terribly quiet. Yet that wasn't true for he could hear the incessant roar of the waves as they broke against the rocks below. So it wasn't actually *quiet* in that sense. But everything was so still.

He went to the window and stared out. He could see the other cottages. Smoke came from two chimneys but there was no sign of life. The sea was rough, huge white flecked waves racing in. Everything was so still. Nothing was happening. Nothing. And he was used to such a different life. A life that was one long mad rush, trying to get sixty hours work into a day; a life in which he met people all the time, had personal contact with them, was involved with them and now . . .

Six months of hibernation. Six months of *killing time*. Six months of doing nothing. How on earth was he going to endure it?

He bent down and took off his wet shoes and socks and then relaxed . . .

Someone was shaking him. He woke up and found Gillian bending over him. There was a delicious smell of fried onions. He saw that she had changed into a yellow frock with a dark

13

blue cardigan.

'You've been asleep for three hours, good!' she told him, just as if he was a small child, 'that'll make you feel better. Anyhow it gave me time to get things straight. Don't move and I'll bring you in something to eat.'

She darted away like a small sparrow and in a moment was back, staggering under a heavy tray that she put down before him. A bowl of thick tomato soup; a covered plate of fried sausages, onions and chips, and a strong cup of coffee.

'How can I thank you . . .' he began.

'By enjoying it,' she told him, curling up in one of the arm-chairs and smiling. 'That's the best thanks a cook can get.'

He began to eat. He hadn't realized just how hungry he was! 'It's delicious.'

Gillian laughed. 'Well, that's good. I've put a bottle in your bed, for you look to me as if you're getting or have got the 'flu. There are eggs in the kitchen, bread, butter, and marmalade. Oh, and a cereal. Hope it's the one you like. You boil an egg for breakfast by putting it in cold water, letting it come to the boil and let it boil for three minutes. Least that's the way I do it. Some people like it softer, some harder. You'll just have to experiment. See you tomorrow . . .'

Even as he tried to speak, she was gone. As he heard the sound of her car dying away he drank the coffee gratefully and felt new life surge through him. He took the tray to the kitchen and glanced out of the window at the desolate garden.

He could see lights in the windows of the other cottages, some of which had been turned into two-storey houses. Why on earth did people choose to live here he asked himself. Of all the miserable places . . .

Sitting down before the fire again, he wondered what on earth he was going to do with the hours—the empty hours—that lay ahead. He yawned. The first day of his new strange life was nearly over. He yawned again and fell asleep.

He woke up hours later. The fire was out save for a few glowing embers. Yawning, he went to the bedroom, hastily undressing and climbing into the big bed, amazingly grateful for the welcoming warmth of the hot water bottle. Even as he fell asleep again, he was smiling. How very different this was from his old life. If David Rugg and his wife could see him how they would laugh!

CHAPTER THREE

Gillian was busy in the stables as the sun came out with a watery look from behind the grey clouds. She hummed as she worked and kept an eye through the open stable door on her three dogs. She loved the smell of the horses, the sound of their breath, the touch of them. She was happy. There was only one thing worrying her.

Had she made a mistake that morning? Would Peter Richardson be annoyed with her? Perhaps even think she was chasing him?

She went outside into the cool sea breeze with a rueful smile. If only she wasn't so concerned about people. Peter Richardson had looked absolutely exhausted the night before. Not only that but utterly miserable. It wasn't natural or right for a man of his age, and his obvious position—for you don't own a Bentley if you're a poor man!—to look like that. There was something wrong. Something very wrong.

After her breakfast and the departure of her parents for their respective jobs in Cudjack, she had gone up to Puffin Cottage and let herself in quietly. Mrs. Trent had given her a spare key once, 'In case one of our relatives lose ours!' she'd said. The cottage had been quiet but she could hear Peter Richardson's deep breathing so she had moved quietly round the kitchen, washing up the dirty dishes, preparing the breakfast, laying the table, then slipping into the front room and laying and lighting the fire. He had still been asleep when she left the cottage and it had worried her ever since. Maybe she should have stayed away? Maybe he would be annoyed, even upset.

Would he think she was trying to intrude, or even trespass on his privacy? Obviously he wanted to be left alone and—even more obviously—he was quite incapable of looking after himself.

Now, as she called to the dogs they came leaping excitedly for it was time for their daily exercise along the sands, racing, running in circles, exploring all the time.

Gillian walked slowly, her eyes dreamy. There was certainly something very wrong with poor Mr. Richardson, she was thinking. He was a bad liar. The tips of his ears had gone bright red when he said he was going to write a book. Gillian's father's ears did exactly the same and it was a family joke that he always gave himself away. Why had Mr. Richardson told a lie? Why did he want to be alone? And what was a well-dressed man like that doing here in March, of all seasons?

She scuffled through the sand, clambered over the rocks, threw pebbles for the three dogs, and went on worrying about the man who still lay peacefully asleep, high up on the cliffside.

He was unhappy! That was obvious. He hated the cottage, the district and the next six months! That was also obvious. But why? Had his wife just died and was he mourning for her? Or had she walked out on him? Perhaps that would be even more painful. To love someone and be rejected by them. Or was he in some sort of trouble? Had he perhaps done something wrong and was he hiding from the police?

She stood still, shocked, running her hand through her short hair. No. Most definitely no, she said aloud, and the dogs turned to look, startled, at her.

No, Peter Richardson wasn't like that. He was a good man. She was sure of that. There must be some other reason.

All the same, it was *his* life and she had no right to keep bursting in on him. If he wanted to be alone, she should let him be alone. Sometimes that was the best medicine you could have, she told herself sternly.

She stifled a sigh but made up her mind. She would leave him alone. The next move must come from him. She would take the dogs home and drive into Cudjack, change her library books, look in and see her mother, who was Chief Librarian, then pop along to the surgery and see her father, who was the local vet and do some shopping. That would keep her out of the way so that Peter Richardson could be alone.

When Peter awoke, he was shocked to see it was eleven o'clock. Eleven o'clock. He hadn't slept as late as that for years!

He began to leap out of bed and then realized that he could stay in bed all day long if he wanted to do so. It no longer mattered. It gave him a strange feeling. A kind of aimlessness, a feeling of no longer being needed, of no longer being—perhaps?—important.

All the same, he couldn't stay in bed all day. Besides that nice kid might turn up again and what would she think of him, lazily lying in bed!

He got up and explored the bathroom and found there was a calor gas geyser and had a bath. He looked at his clothes as he unpacked them all and he gave a lop-sided grin. How unsuitable they were! Dark, elegantly cut suits. Bowler hat. Umbrella. He tried to imagine himself strolling along the sands, twirling his umbrella.

The thought sent him with a wry smile to the kitchen. He stopped dead in the doorway with surprise for the table was laid with his favourite cereal—how had she known that? An egg and two slices of bacon were in a frying pan waiting on the cooker. On the table was a slim glass vase with two golden daffodils in it.

Gillian! What a nice kid she was. He cooked his breakfast carefully and ate it enjoyably. This salt air certainly gave him an appetite, he thought. One thing, having breakfast so late meant he could miss out lunch.

He washed up, finding it difficult to know where to put everything but determined to learn so that when Gillian next came along, she wouldn't find a hopeless mess!

Then he went outside. The sun was trying to

shine. Bravely but not very successfully, he thought, as he looked at the vast expanse of ocean. Grey water with huge rollers racing in with their patient, dogmatic fury. He glanced round him curiously, more interested now than he had been the previous day when he had been tired. The cottages on either side of him looked empty; probably waiting for the season to begin and the rush of holiday-makers. Then he saw a wisp of smoke from the lower cottage which looked slightly bigger than the others. The windows had net curtains. Why? he wondered, for there were no passers-by to gaze inquisitively in the windows. And if there were, did it really matter? He had a *thing* about net curtains and venetian blinds, and thought they should be done away with, except in towns where traffic and crowds made privacy otherwise impossible.

He strolled round the garden. It was a sorry sight, as the girl had said. However, it could hardly be expected that Amelia Rugg's cousin, Mrs. Trent, could pop down here from Cheltenham to look after the garden. Temporary tenants were not likely to show interest in planting flowers they would never see bloom. They could hardly be expected to . . .

His thoughts jerked to a standstill as his mind questioned that statement. Any why not? You couldn't spend your life confining yourself to tasks that you would profit by or see the end of, could you? Surely the knowledge that the fruits of your labour would give pleasure to another at some later date should be reward enough? It was a thought that had never occurred to him before. Yet it was true, wasn't it?

It was so still. Not quiet, of course, with the incessant roar of the ocean but so still! So dead! Lonely. He went indoors, suddenly unable to bear it.

Used, as he was, to the sound of jet planes zooming overhead, the impatient cacophony of horns as the long, tortured lines of cars waited to move, the high, shouting voices that were necessary if you were to conduct a conversation as you walked along the crowded pavements, this quietness seemed strange, eerie, almost as if he had left this world and been transported to another. A life on another planet, so to speak.

He wandered aimlessly round the cottage, talking to himself. In a way, wasn't that what had happened? He was going to have to lead a completely different life for the next six months—at least. He had to rebuild his life. Everything was so different. How could he possibly endure six months of doing nothing? Yet he had no choice. As David had truthfully pointed out, on the day he told him he'd let the flat to the man who was to take his place.

Peter suddenly remembered how he had told Gillian he was going to write a book.

21

Maybe he should write one? But what about? And how? He hadn't a clue . . .

He decided to drive into the nearest town and buy some clothes. Something that didn't look so ridiculous as his dark suits!

He drove down the hill, then past the large, expensive-looking houses that lined the front, then past the small group of avant-garde shops that obviously served this Cornish 'suburbia', the only old building being the small sub-post office, and over the old stone narrow bridge into the small village of Trevennon built in a valley by the side of the river Nonn. He looked at the signpost and wondered at the strange name of Cudjack. It looked as if that was the nearest town.

When he reached it, Cudjack proved to be a typical market town with a big square and old buildings and a few surprisingly modern shops here and there. He browsed round the men's shop, gazing idly at ties and shirts, aware that he was doing that most incredible of all things: 'killing time'. He had no desire to go back to that desolate empty cottage yet he couldn't wander round indefinitely. Finally he bought two pairs of trousers and a loose black pullover as well as a sports jacket. Also some tougher shoes and three drip-dry shirts for it looked as if he'd have to do his own laundry, now!

He stopped at the bookshop and bought some paperback thrillers, then saw the amazingly modern-looking library. He went in and enquired about joining the library and was given all the details by a tall, thin, blonde-haired woman who looked at him with frank curiosity.

'You'll find it very quiet out there . . .' she was saying 'Why, Mr. Richardson . . . what a bit of luck . . .' a voice interrupted. Peter swung round instantly, recognizing the lilt in the voice.

'Gillian . . .' he used her Christian name without thinking. 'What are you doing here?'

She laughed. She was wearing a pale green tweed suit with a matching beret on the back of her head. 'I came to see Mum. She's librarian here, you know.'

'I didn't know . . .' He realized he was absurdly glad to see her. 'I say . . . I missed out on lunch. How about some coffee?'

'Super . . .' Gillian laughed. 'On one condition.'

'Fair's fair. What must I do?'

'Give me a lift home. I drove in but my car's got something wrong with it and I had to leave it at the garage. I thought I'd have to hang around for Mum or Dad, so it's a bit of luck meeting you . . .'

'And that's no lie . . .' he said, as he led the way out of the modern building.

Gillian turned with a smile. 'What was that?'

He laughed. 'Nothing.' Yet it had been the

23

truth. He *had* thought it a bit of luck meeting her. Like a ray of sunshine on a wet day! What a corny thought, he told himself, but true. This loneliness, this strange aimlessness, was getting him down. He was so unused to it but no doubt in time . . .

They chatted as they sat in the low-ceilinged, timbered room, eating scones with jam and cream, drinking cups of coffee.

Gillian told him about her parents. 'They both work and love it, you see, so they're always out. In the evenings, they always play bridge . . .'

'So you're alone?'

'I'm used to it . . .' Gillian took another scone, looked guilty and then laughed. 'I'm lucky—I never put on weight. I read a lot, have T.V. and have got masses of friends.'

'I bet you have . . .' Peter said thoughtfully, then looked up. 'You love people, don't you, Gillian?'

She went bright red. 'I'm not a Do-Gooder . . .' she said quickly.

It was his turn to be embarrassed. 'I wasn't implying that. Simply that you love helping people. You get kicks from it, don't you? I mean, it was awfully good of you to come up and get my breakfast ready. I didn't wake up until eleven o'clock . . .'

He saw she was relaxing. 'You didn't mind?'

'Mind? Are you mad? Of course I didn't mind. I thought it was very kind of you. I still

24

feel a bit lost . . .'

She nodded. 'You look a bit lost. It's so different from your ordinary life?'

He sighed, twirled a spoon round slowly; 'And how! Still—I'll learn to live with it. Just takes time. There's nothing to do. That's what's driving me round the bend. Nothing to do but kill time . . .'

She hastily finished eating and suggested they go. He wanted something to do, did he? Well, she thought, with a smile, that shouldn't be too hard to find!

He drove her home, commenting as he drove through the typical fishing village of Trevonnen how surprised he'd been when he came to what he called 'suburbia'.

'You mean Pendennis?' Gillian said with a laugh. 'Well, we are quite separate from Trevonnen. They don't accept us. You know what Cornish folk are like—even when you've lived here forty years you're still a "furriner".'

She laughed again. 'It seems that a bright speculator bought the land and decided to build what some call the "stockbroker class" of houses. They sold immediately like hot cakes.'

But who on earth could want to live in Pendennis?'

Gillian looked puzzled. 'I do. Lots of us do. It's quite nice when you know it.'

'But . . .'

They had reached the small modern block of shops and were now approaching the first of the big houses. 'We could be anywhere. Esher, Weybridge, anywhere near London. Somehow it looks all wrong with the beach and sea so near.'

'Why not? Look over there, that's a school. Co-Educational and boarding school ...' Gillian said. 'I wanted to go but Dad said, "No, but definitely no ..."' She laughed happily. 'He's an awful square, bless him. "Time enough to meet boys when you're old enough to cope with them," he told me.' She chuckled. 'If he did but know. We all had boy friends, naturally.'

'Naturally?' Peter was uncomfortably aware that his voice sounded stiff. He saw the quick amused glance Gillian gave him and realized that in her eyes, he was as old and as square as her father.

He dropped her off at her house and found himself admiring it and the beautiful garden ablaze with red tulips and daffodils as well as primroses, golden under the trees which were beginning to show buds.

'Soon be Spring,' Gillian said cheerfully as she said goodbye and hurried to the dogs who were racing madly to greet her. A red setter, a Great Dane and an Alsatian.

'Soon?' Peter asked himself as he drove slowly towards the hated cottage. What was 'soon' he wondered.

26

CHAPTER FOUR

It was absurd, Peter Richardson knew, but he felt a vague disappointment next morning when he went out to the kitchen and found only the dirty plates from his dinner the night before. Somehow he had thought Gillian would have come . . .

On the other hand, he could hardly expect her to do so, could he? She had her own busy, if aimless, life to lead. He stifled a sigh and boiled an egg. Not very successfully for it was watery and he loathed watery eggs. Doubtless in time, he told himself, he would learn.

The quietness of the cottage oppressed him. The evening before had seemed endless, sitting in front of the fire, pretending to read but most of the time, he had been thinking with an almost overwhelming depression of the long empty months ahead of him. How could he endure them?

At least the sun was shining. After he had washed up, he went outside and looked at the suddenly blue sea. The air was very clear and there was a thin, dark blue line on the horizon. He decided to go for a walk. That would pass the time!

He walked up the road that led towards the top of the cliff, perhaps two hundred yards above. The cold wind blew at him but he was wearing his new polo necked pullover, and in a way the wind was refreshing. He paused, breathing deeply, smelling the ozone, filling his lungs with the coldness.

He glanced curiously at the cottage above him as he passed it for it was obviously empty with the rather drab mustard-yellow curtains drawn but the garden was well-attended, crowded as it was with small purple and orange crocuses and daffodils tossing their gold heads in the wind. He looked back at Puffin Cottage's garden and sighed. It certainly did look desolate but he wasn't interested in gardening and had no desire to work in it.

The empty cottage was the last one and above it, the road dwindled away to a mere track so that he walked through the rough yellowish grass, past the gorse bushes. It was quite a climb to the top of the hill and the wind grew fiercer and colder the higher he went. At the top, he paused, catching his breath at the different picture before him.

Thanks be, he thought, his cottage was on the other side, even though it was desolate and lonely. This side there was a vast caravan camp. He shuddered as he imagined the noise and chaos during the holiday season. Line after line of regimented brightly-painted caravans, all merging on a large central building, where there was obviously a cafeteria, plus the necessary 'Mod cons'. Further along, past the caravans, were rows and rows of neat little chalets, these were also built round a large motel.

It all looked deserted and rather pathetic on this windy March day but he visualized what it would be like when the holidays began! He wouldn't be here, of course, he started to think but his thoughts slid to a frightening halt. For he would be! Until September 'at least'. He only hoped the holiday makers would keep to their side of the hill!

He had begun to walk again but stopped dead, startled at the selfishness of his thoughts. Also the inconsistency. Hadn't he been silently moaning because his side of the hill was so silent, so empty of life? What did he want? You can't have your cake and eat it, he told himself sternly, and found himself grinning at his own corniness. Help, he told himself, if you're like this on your second day, heaven help you after six months of it!

Walking down towards the camp he noticed how well designed it was and could imagine the laughter, the shouts, the rushing about of the children and he certainly hoped for everyone's sake, it would be a good summer. He climbed over a low stone wall and was in the camp—here there was every kind of commercial means to make the holiday-makers happy. Play parks with all sorts of intriguing climbing and swinging gadgets. A Bingo Hall. A large swimming pool for those who feared the waves.

Finally he reached the beach. This was a much bigger cove than the one on the other side and it had fascinating piles of rocks and exciting little pools in which there were tiny crabs and fish. There was no sign of human life, not even a curling wisp of blue smoke from a chimney, so he thrust his hands deep in his pockets, and walked back along the wet sands.

The tide was far out and he reckoned he had time before it came in to walk round the cliff to the beach at 'suburbia'. He wondered what would happen if the two locales ever overlapped.

He walked slowly, remembering his childhood for it was years since he had walked along the sands and then he had clung to his Grannie's hand, a bit scared of the big white waves that seemed to be chasing him. His parents had been abroad as usual. They were in the diplomatic service and there was no room for a small boy in their lives. Thanks to Gran, he had a more or less normal childhood, but he could still remember his feeling of rejection on Speech Days when he enviously watched the other boys with their proud parents and he had no one, for his Gran had died by then, and he spent his holidays at school. However, he thought as he walked round a seaweed-covered rock, it had taught him to walk alone, to avoid being involved with other people, to be wary of getting hurt. He was like Kipling's cat, he thought, with a rueful smile. He had complete control of his emotions and he needed no one . . . No one at all!

As he rounded the corner, he saw how high the tide would come up and he doubted if the holiday makers from the caravan camp would often venture round. He hoped not—and then was shocked by his own selfishness and the way he was beginning to see this cove as *his*.

It was a small cove with the river turning into an estuary before it joined the sea. He could see the small houses of the village in the valley huddled together and nearer his cottage—*his*, again?—the big expensive-looking houses, one of which was Gillian's . . .

His feet sinking into the dry sand, he struggled up the beach to the road, and began to walk home. *Home?* he thought. Was he adjusting himself already? He glanced at his watch. Normally he'd be driving round having coped with his first surgery, and he'd be planning ahead for the rest of the day. An endless round of rushing madly, pausing to look calm and with plenty of time to hear the symptoms of each patient, and then another mad rush to the next port of call. How very different from this! Was it only as early as that, he thought with dismay as he saw the time. How on earth would he get through the day?

He walked by the houses, gazing curiously and without any inhibitions at them for if he had to live near these people for the next six months, he must be wary. A bachelor in a small community could find himself enveloped in a web of boring social life. He decided to hide the fact that he played bridge, otherwise he'd spend every evening playing, and although he enjoyed it, he liked to play with good if not better players than himself. He could imagine the type of people who lived here! He paused before a stone wall that separated the beautiful garden from the pavement and gently tickled a small white kitten who purred happily. It was a big house, built in pseudo-Tudor style.

The door opened, and a short, plump, grey-haired woman in a blue frock with an apron came hurrying out. She grabbed the kitten and held her tightly, gazing angrily up at Peter, almost accusingly as if he'd been about to kidnap the small white kitten.

'Twiggy,' she scolded. 'You belong up here and if aught happens ...' she began saying angrily but her voice changed as her face lost its hostile look and crinkled into a smile. 'Oh, Sir, you must be the Mr. Richardson ...' she said almost delightedly. 'I do hope as you'll be happy here, Sir. And if you wish, I can come along and clean you up but I can't stay and cook your meals.'

Peter smiled. 'I know, Miss ...' he frowned. What on earth was Gillian's surname? Somehow he had only thought of her as

Gillian, never as a Miss anyone.

'She told you, did she?' The stout little woman beamed. 'I know how it is with you genelmen for you just don't know what to do. I'll pop in and make your bed, wash up and lay the fire ready first thing every morning so it's all nice and clean.'

'That'll be fine.'

Old Kitty beamed and, still grabbing the kitten, hurried into the house, closing the door with a last quick farewell smile and bob of her head.

Peter strolled on, wondering what sort of people lived in these houses. The next one was Gillian's. More of a rambling type as if bits had been added but the garden was really beautiful. The print of the horses' hooves were plain on the muddy drive so he imagined she had gone out riding. There was no sound of the dogs who always followed her wherever she went.

He was walking by when he did suddenly hear an excited barking, and the red Setter, the Great Dane and the Alsatian all came racing round the house towards him, followed by Gillian, in skimpy blue jeans with a red blouse and matching red scarf round her head. Her feet were bare.

'Solak . . .' she shouted, 'Rex . . . Little . . .'

The dogs seemed to halt in mid-air, turned round and hurried back to her obediently. It made Peter smile for she was such a bit of a girl and looked so frail, yet the dogs' delighted leaps at her failed to knock her down and Peter, from experience, knew just how matter-of-fact and efficient she could be.

'How did the breakfast go?' she asked him politely but her eyes were laughing.

'Badly,' he confessed. 'A horrible watery egg.'

She laughed outright. 'I did warn you. Double the seconds you allowed it. You'll learn—'

'In time,' he finished ruefully.

'I've been writing out some simple recipes but I doubt if you'll need them. Everyone's thrilled to hear we have a writer with us and you'll be positively overwhelmed with invitations.'

'I was afraid of that . . .' he began and saw her frown.

'Don't tell me you're an introvert. You can't be for writers simply have to know people, don't they?'

He hadn't thought of it, before. Not being a writer, he had no idea! He was beginning to regret his lie.

'In a way but . . .'

'Course you need time to think and to write . . .' Gillian went on gaily, 'But really they're not a bad lot here, you know. I think you'll get a lot of material . . .'

'Material?' he echoed, puzzled.

He saw her look of surprise. 'Yes, material.

Isn't that what you call ideas and plots and things?'

Laughing, he agreed. 'Yes—if you call it anything.'

'I spoke to old Kitty . . .'

'Thanks. I saw her just now.'

'Of course . . . She works for the Oswalds today. How's the 'flu?'

'It seems to have gone. I feel better. Just had a walk along the beach.'

'That'll do you good . . .' Gillian told him gravely. 'I bet in your normal life you don't walk at all except to your car.'

Normal life. The words struck him and he looked quickly at her, but her face was innocent and he realized that she must, of course, know that a man of his age wouldn't normally have time to wander aimlessly over wet sand!

'I must admit I'm not a keen walker,' he agreed.

'You will be,' she promised. 'There's something fascinating about the sea. By the way, d'you ride?' He nodded and she smiled. 'Goody. I've got a new horse, Walkabout, who might suit you. He needs exercise and doesn't get enough with only me to ride them all at the moment so please do come down whenever you feel like it. I have a groom, old Brummel . . .' She smiled and her eyes sparkled. 'We call him that because he looks ghastly all the week but on Sundays he spruces up as he's courting.' She chuckled. 'He's nearer seventy than sixty and he's been courting the same woman for fifty years. Maybe one day he'll pop the question.'

'Perhaps he's not the marrying sort.'

Gillian laughed. 'I guess he isn't. You're not, are you?' she asked, startling him, and then made it worse by adding, 'You're scared of being hurt.'

'What on earth makes you say that?' He knew he sounded annoyed, but he couldn't help it for he was shocked.

'I'm sorry,' she said but he knew she wasn't. He knew she had said it deliberately. 'It stands out a mile, Peter.'

It was the first time she had used his Christian name and he had a strange feeling that it was a gesture of friendliness, the admittance of a desire to help him.

She turned away, speaking over her shoulder. 'How about having some lunch with me? Ham, salad and plenty of cheese. How about it?'

He hesitated. 'If I'm not a nuisance.'

Gillian laughed. 'Of course not. It's much more fun eating with someone . . .' She led the way down the drive towards the house. 'Don't worry, Peter. We'll have a chaperone, Alice, my old Nanny, lives with us.'

'You make me sound an awful square . . .' he protested.

Gillian turned quickly and smiled up at him.

36

'I didn't mean to, Peter. I think you're a honey and you're going to do us all a lot of good.'

Peter spoke quickly, 'I'm here to . . .'

She tucked her hand through his arm. 'I know and I promise I won't forget it. You're here to write a book! All the same, you have to meet people to write about them and we surely have a weird crowd here. We'll seem like creatures from another sphere.'

She looked up at him, her elf-like face amused but her eyes serious. 'Honestly Peter, we have our problems. Not MY family, luckily. As you know Dad's a vet and loves it and Mum loves her work, too. Week-ends they play golf and bridge and they're about the happiest couple I know. But some of our neighbours . . . Boy, are they in a mess!'

Peter frowned. 'You're very interested in people.'

'Of course. I love them and I want to know what makes them tick and I like to help them with their problems . . .' she said eagerly, watching his face, and her own suddenly clouded over. 'I don't interfere though. I'm not a Do-Gooder.' She hesitated. 'Don't you find people interesting?'

It was a difficult question to answer. As he considered it, he realized that he had acquired the habit of not seeing people as *people*. The conveyor-belt routine of modern surgery, when so much had to be learned about the patient in as short a time as possible, had destroyed the old-fashioned Family Physician, and his notes told him what he needed to know but he realized suddenly that, out of all his many regular patients, he knew very little about them as *people*.

Not that he had ever wanted to know about them, of course. He had early learned to avoid involvement or anything personal. It was the same as when an operation was performed, the patient ceased to be a person. Peter realized that that was how he saw his patients. Not as people but as numbers on their cards.

They'd walked round the back now and he saw the cobbled yard and the stables. Several horses had their heads out, gazing at them, and the dogs went racing down a wide track towards a part of the garden that must be the paddock.

Gillian led the way to the back door. 'It's easier this way,' she said cheerfully.

The kitchen was large and copper saucepans shone in the sunshine. He saw a washing machine, a big refrigerator, a well-scrubbed table and chairs, and a tall thin woman at the sink.

As she turned, she stared at him warily, almost as Old Kitty had done, as if he threatened them or someone they loved.

'Nanny,' Gillian was saying, 'this is Mr. Richardson who has taken Puffin Cottage for six months. He's staying for lunch. There's heaps, isn't there?'

The thin woman with greying hair smiled politely. 'I guessed you'd be asking him, Gillian, when I saw you outside talking so I've made some soup. Cold ham and salad's not much of a meal for a guest.'

Gilliam laughed. 'He isn't a guest, Nanny, he's a friend. Thanks all the same. It smells super. Come on, Peter. Like a drink?'

She led the way through the hall to a small room. There was a large picture window looking on to the smooth lawn and across the road to the beach and sea. It gave a feeling of limitless space and made the room seem bigger than it was. He glanced round curiously for it was bright with colours that were almost crazy in their daring provocative shades. Small cushions of red, green, blue, yellow and even purple were tossed on the divan that was covered by an enormous black lace shawl. There were strange vividly-coloured paintings on the wall, a deep red carpet, cream silk curtains, Gillian switched on a transistor so that the room was filled with pop music.

'This is my room,' Gillian said proudly. 'Mum's rooms are so stuffy. Take a pew. I've got some brandy, or whisky if you prefer it.'

'Brandy please . . .' Peter sank into a weird-looking armchair. It was made in a complete circle into which you sank but that was surprisingly comfortable once you got used to it. Gillian might be twenty but the room looked as if she was still an adolescent teenager, he thought.

She poured the drinks—he noted she only had orange squash—and then she curled up on the divan. 'Okay?' she asked with a smile.

He smiled back. 'Okay.' He sipped his drink slowly.

It was just the way he liked it. She was an odd girl—always getting things right.

'You're not married?' Gillian asked abruptly, her eyes interested but her voice casual.

'No—nor likely to be,' he told her.

'Famous last words.' She jumped up and went to the window. 'Isn't it gorgeous? I hate being shut in. This is so . . . so open. Nothing constricting . . .'

'Marriage can be . . .'

She turned to look at him. 'Can be?'

'Constricting.'

Smiling she shook her head. 'Not if you're sensible. Mum and Dad are happy. They share interests, both have busy lives.'

'You think it's a good thing for a wife to have a career?'

'Oh, definitely, if she wants one.'

'But you won't?'

She shook her head again. 'I'll be too busy.'

'Doing what?'

The question seemed to surprise her. 'Loving my husband, of course, and looking after our children.'

40

A gong sounded and she took his empty glass. 'Time to eat. Nanny's soup is something special and she gets hurt if we let it cool.'

The dining-room was impressive. And totally characterless Peter thought, glancing round at the walnut table gleaming with polish, the perfect glass, the bright silver, the beautifully arranged flowers in the centre. The cream walls matched the brocade curtains. There was a view of the garden bright with colour. He had a feeling that the room had been planned to impress.

Once again Gillian practised her uncanny habit of reading his thoughts.

'Mum hopes one day to have her house in colour in *Vogue* or some such mag. She has an outsize inferiority complex, poor love, and has to impress people.'

'I thought you said she was happy.'

'Oh, she is, Dad's wonderful. He boosts her morale and has made her a different woman. I couldn't care less what people think . . .'

'And that's obvious, Miss Gillian,' Nanny said, her sudden formality plainly showing her righteous disapproval. 'Coming to eat with muddy bare feet and looking a proper mess too, with a guest here and all. I'm ashamed of you, that I am. After all I've taught you. What this nice gentleman must think of you, I hate to imagine.'

Peter half-expected Gillian to laugh but instead she went bright red and apologized.

'Sorry, Nanny, I forgot. Honest I did. I won't be a moment, Peter . . .'

She vanished from the room and Peter sat down as the tall thin woman brought him a coral-coloured plate of soup.

'How old is she really?' he asked.

Alice gave him a sharp look and then smiled.

'She's twenty all right, Mr. Richardson, sir, and you can check that at Somerset House, but there are times when I think she's less than fourteen. Sometimes I think she doesn't want to grow up . . .' She stopped speaking as Gillian returned, her hair brushed, face clean, slippers on her bare feet, and jeans discarded for a yellow skirt with a brown jersey.

'Are you talking about me?' she asked.

'Any objection?' Peter teased.

'None, so long as it was . . .'

'The truth?'

Gillian laughed. 'I was going to say *kind*.'

'As if I'd say an unkind thing about you, Gillian child. 'Twas the truth we were saying . . .' Nanny said as she left the room.

Gillian lifted her eyebrows as she smiled at Peter.

'I don't know how you did it but you've won old Nanny's heart. She's got high standards and always disapproves of my boy friends.' She laughed, 'Oh, don't look so scared, Peter, you're not one of them. You're much too old. Just how old are you?'

42

Peter hesitated but only for a moment. 'Thirty-five,' he said truthfully, watching her expression. She saw him as a *square* of course. A good thing, for girls of her age were apt to have 'crushes'—and it could be embarrassing in such a small group of people. He had no desire to break the child's heart but he was determined that, as a doctor, he must walk alone.

CHAPTER FIVE

Peter had no desire to walk up the hill to the quiet cottage where he'd be alone so, when he left the Yeltons' house, he strolled towards the Cornish village.

He wandered round the cobbled streets, went to the small harbour, paused to look at the fishing nets hanging out, and walked on aimlessly, aware of cold eyes watching him and remembering what Gillian had said about being considered a 'furriner' even when you've lived there forty years!

Imagine living here for forty years, he thought. Six months was hell enough. What on earth was he going to do with himself? You can only walk for so long . . .

Finally he went home—for there was nothing else to do. He walked hurriedly past the Yelton House, hoping Gillian would see him, yet not wanting her to think he was seeking her out. He had begun to realize that Gillian's company was not only relaxing but provocative for she said the most amazing and disconcerting things at times.

Such, for instance, as when she had said he was not the 'marrying kind' and had added: 'You're too scared.'

Was that true? he wondered. Was he scared of marriage? If so, why? There was only one reason why he didn't want to marry—and that was simple enough! because he believed a dedicated doctor should remain single—so that he was completely free to do his work.

He'd had many married friends whose marriages were broken because of the wife's inability to accept the fact that work comes first. True, he thought, kicking idly at a stone on the path, he had some happily-married doctor friends also, the Ruggs, for instance. They were happy and Amelia never minded when David walked out at a dinner party, or failed to turn up for an anniversary celebration. But then Amelia was an exceptional person. She also had her own work as a social worker that absorbed her. Strictly speaking though, Peter decided as he reached Puffin Cottage, he knew he would be happier single. When you loved someone you became involved and involvement was . . .

His thoughts skidded to a stop as he stared at the door-step, for neatly placed in front of the purple front door, was a spade, a fork, a hoe and two boxes of small green plants.

Oh no! was his first indignant reaction. Why should he work in someone else's garden?

How had the tools got there? he wondered. Gillian must have driven them up. She must have come while he was in the village. Well, if that wasn't the limit! That girl had a nerve. He had no intention of gardening! He loathed the very idea. Inside the cottage he glanced at the clock and groaned aloud. It *must* be later than three o'clock! What on earth was there to do?

He sighed. Gillian had won! There was one thing he could do. He took off his coat and rolled up his sleeves. He'd never been a gardener but it looked as if he might as well begin. At least it would help to pass the time.

When he finished, his back ached and his hands had blisters. Finished? he asked himself with an ironic smile. Why, he'd hardly scraped the surface of the soil. It was hard and dry from the salty winds. Examining the plants carefully he wondered what they were, then found a tiny piece of wood and printed on it was the word: LOBELIA.

As he scrubbed his hands and looked ruefully at them, he tried to remember what a 'lobelia' was. He had a vague idea it was a blue flower. He had started work on the front garden but it would take him weeks to get it looking anything like a garden! How his back ached! and tomorrow he'd be stiff from using

45

muscles he'd allowed to get lazy. Maybe a hot bath . . .

There was a gentle tap on the front door. Peter opened it and a small boy with ginger hair, freckled nose and a big grin held out an envelope.

'Please Sir, they want an answer, Sir . . .' he said cheerfully.

'Just a moment, then,' Peter said and ripped open the envelope. The letter was brief and to the point.

'My husband and I would be delighted if you'd come to dinner tonight. Gillian has told us about you and a new face is always welcome here. Can we expect you about seven o'clock?' It was signed *Anne Yelton*.

'Come in,' Peter told the boy. 'I'll just write an answer. What's your name?'

The boy grinned. 'I'm called Ginger . . .'

Peter smiled. 'I'm not surprised but what's your real name?'

The boy's face changed. He looked almost sullen. He fidgeted, rubbing one foot against his leg. 'Archibald . . .' he said.

'Oh no!' Peter murmured. 'You poor little devil.'

The boy looked surprised. 'I thought you'd laugh. Most people do.'

Peter laughed, then, 'Not me. I was

christened Peter Edward Arthur Richardson. That spells pear so I was called Fruity at school. It used to make me mad. Many's the fight I've had over that. I just wish parents would think about their children when they choose their name.'

Ginger looked happier. 'You fought them when they called you Fruity?'

'And how! What do they call you?'

Ginger fidgeted again. 'Artichoke.'

'Tough luck but that's the way it is,' Peter said, 'one day it'll be Baldy. Do you fight them?'

Ginger grinned. 'I'd like to but I always lose. I'm little, you see . . .'

Peter nodded. He did see for the boy was thin and pale.

'Little people always have to be aggressive, I'm afraid.'

'I am aggressive,' Ginger said proudly, 'or so Jacquie says. She gets awful mad at me when I come home bleeding.'

'Jacquie?'

'She's my sister but she's sort of a Mum, too. Our Mum died four years ago, you see, and Jacquie looks after us.'

'I see.' Peter looked at the small boy thoughtfully. 'Ever thought of learning Judo?'

The boy's face brightened. 'You bet. There's a class in Cudjack but Jacquie won't let me go. She says I'm too young and how'd I get there?' He looked up at Peter, his face suddenly hopeful. 'Maybe you'd like to go to the classes, too, then we could go together? Jacquie wouldn't mind then.'

Peter was startled. 'What, me go to Judo classes?'

Ginger's smile was sympathetic. 'You scared? I am too, but I'd be all right with you there. Would you . . . ?'

Peter ran his finger round his collar. This was getting a bit too much. 'Well, look, I'll make some enquiries about it . . .' he said evasively. Somehow he'd have to think up an escape route.

'Gillian knows all about it,' Ginger informed him triumphantly. 'You ask her. She'll fix it for us. She goes every week.'

'Gillian does?' Peter sighed with relief. 'Then you can go with her.'

Ginger shook his head. 'Oh no, I can't. Jacquie says that Gillian does too much for us all and that I mustn't be a nuisance. I wouldn't be a nuisance to you, would I?'

Peter sighed helplessly for Ginger had the appealing eyes of a spaniel. 'Well, look, I'll talk to Gillian about it and . . .'

Ginger gave a little skip. 'Oh, boy, is that super . . .' He turned to go but Peter stopped him.

'Hey, young fellow, I've got to give you an answer to this note . . .' He re-read the invitation. His first reaction had been to politely refuse it. He didn't want to get caught up in a round of dinners—nor had he felt much like it after his afternoon in the garden. But now ... he had a few things to say to Gillian Yelton!

Quickly he found some paper and wrote a hasty acceptance. 'Sorry there's no envelope but I haven't one,' he wrote at the end, folded it and gave it to Ginger. He also gave him several pence.

'Boy ... oh boy ...' Ginger skipped happily. 'Am I glad you've come here, Mr. Richardson. Gillian said I would be ...'

He had darted off before Peter could say anything. Peter watched the small boy racing down the hillside and then went indoors, his face thoughtful.

Gillian had said that, had she? So Gillian had planned it all—first the gardening, now judo! of all the ... he was about to explode with anger but found himself laughing instead.

Glancing at his watch, he saw he'd have to hurry. He must have a hot bath first ... Just wait until he saw Gillian. This was going too far.

Always a stickler for punctuality, Peter was pleased to see by his watch that it was exactly seven o'clock as he parked his car in front of the Yeltons' front door. He pulled the long old-fashioned bell, deciding that it was best to be formal at this stage and not go in the back way although Gillian had said that was the easiest.

Gillian opened the door, a friendly smile on her face.

'I'm so glad you came. I was afraid you might be too tired.'

'Tired?' he moved stiffly. 'That's no lie, either, Gillian, I'm going to be even worse tomorrow. Look, I wish you'd . . .'

She closed the door, laughing, giving him no chance to finish his sentence. 'You'll get used to it. It's just that you're out of training. I bet you never walk in London.'

'On the contrary,' he began.

Gillian was wearing a pretty pink sheath frock and her hair was a mass of dark curls. As if she read his thoughts, she laughed up at him.

'Don't you like my new wig? I think it's smashing but Dad nearly went off the deep end.'

'I can't make out why you girls wear wigs . . .' Peter admitted. 'It's sort of cheating.'

Gillian laughed. 'Men wear toupees. Do you . . . ?'

Instinctively Peter's hand flew to his forehead. His hair was receding with uncomfortable speed, he had often thought.

'I'm not that old,' he began indignantly.

'Age has nothing to do with it, Peter, some men go bald at twenty.' She was taking off his coat and hat, hanging them up, talking all the time. Now she looked down the hall carefully and then turned to him.

'Peter . . .' she said in a whisper. 'I'm
50

warning you. Mum will be trying to matchmake but don't let it frighten you . . .'

'Matchmake?'

She laughed. 'I knew you'd be scared. I promise you there's no need to worry. I am not chasing you. In any case our age gap is enormous.'

'Fifteen years,' he told her, his voice rather stiff. Was thirty-five so very old? he wondered.

She smiled. 'I know, it's a terrific difference but poor Mum really can't help it. She's always trying to find me a good husband.'

'But she doesn't even know me.'

'That's what I said and she told me that anyone Mrs. Trent knew must be all right.'

'But I don't know Mrs. Trent. She's Amelia's cousin and . . .'

Gillian tucked her hand through his arm—just as if she was his niece, he thought, oddly annoyed, and led the way down the wide hall. 'I know. That's what I said but Mum can't get over the fact that you've wormed your way into the hearts of both Nanny and old Kitty. She thinks if *they* like you, you must be all right.'

She smiled up at him, her slanting eyes amused. 'Now not to worry, Peter, I promise you you're quite safe and Nanny has cooked her special dinner for you.'

Opening the door, she led the way into a long room that seemed to him to be a mass of contradictions. The curtains were of golden silk, the carpet soft, deep, and dark green. On the walls were oil paintings of sombre Dutch scenes. There were flowers everywhere. Great vases of daffodils and narcissi, small bowls of yellow crocuses. But the couch and the arm-chairs were old-fashioned with blue covers. It was as if part of the room was designed to create an impression and the other part was for their comfort.

Gillian smiled at him and he knew that she understood exactly what he was feeling but as she began to speak he saw her mother had followed them into the room, her hand held out.

'Mr. Richardson. I'm so glad you could come at such short notice. We're delighted to meet you . . .'

Mrs. Yelton was a tall, broad-shouldered woman, a little on the stout side but well-corseted. Elegantly dressed in a dark blue lace frock, her smokey-blue hair elaborately waved, she had a warm smile.

'So nice to see a new face . . .' Mrs. Yelton went on, 'And so nice for little Gillian to meet someone like you. It's a very bad place here for young people, you know, Mr. Richardson, Gillian has so few friends . . .'

Peter saw Gillian's mouth open and then close and at that moment a tall, very thin man with tanned face and white hair came to join them.

'Glad to meet you,' he said gruffly but his handshake was warm and his face friendly.

'Now what will you have to drink?'

It proved to be a pleasant evening and Peter enjoyed himself. The only snag was that he had to watch what he said for Gillian's father was a veterinary surgeon and Peter could easily have betrayed his own status as a doctor by the comments he wanted to make. But David Rugg was right, Peter decided. It was best for no one to realize his profession if this was to be the complete change and relaxation he needed. They sat round a log fire, talking, and Peter thought they were two nice people but he sympathized with Gillian's discomfort when her mother kept dropping small hints that Peter would be welcome whenever he liked to call.

'Look upon this as your second home, Peter . . .' she said with a smile. 'I may call you that? Gillian has so few friends unfortunately.'

Later, when Gillian walked out with him to his car, she apologized again.

Peter laughed. 'Don't worry, Gillian, mothers are like that, I understand.'

'Was your mother?'

'I wouldn't know. She died before I left school—and my father. In a car crash.'

'Oh, how awful, Peter.'

'Yes, it was in a way and in a way it wasn't. You see, I'd never really known them. Dad was in the diplomatic service and they were always abroad so I didn't miss them as much as most kids would for I'd never—as I said—known them. On the other hand, it upset me because I had dreams of one day getting to know Dad really well.'

'Didn't you have anyone when you were young?'

Peter smiled. 'Of course. A very sweet Grannie but then, she, too, died, so I'm used to being on my own.'

She looked up at him, her face thoughtful as she nodded.

'That explains a lot of things.'

'Explains?' Peter frowned. 'What d'you mean?'

He saw the way she hesitated. As if she wanted to tell him something and then decided not to. 'Peter, I wonder if you'd come and ride Walkabout for me tomorrow? He's getting restless and I just can't cope with them all.'

He opened his car door. 'Of course, any time, Gillian. What would suit you best?'

'Seven-thirty?' She saw the startled look on his face and went on quickly: 'I didn't want to disturb your working day . . .'

'My working day?' he was puzzled.

Gillian gave him a strangely thoughtful look and he thought he saw her mouth quiver. 'Yes, your writing, of course.'

'Yes, of course,' he said hastily. 'Very thoughtful of you. I thought seven-thirty might be too early for you.'

'Early . . .' Gillian laughed. He had a feeling she was relieved, as if a difficult moment had been passed successfully. 'I get up at six a.m. every morning. Best part of the day. Got an alarm clock? No? I'll lend you one. Won't be a mo.' She darted back into the house and returned with an alarm clock. 'I've set it for seven because you'll have breakfast when you get back, I expect.'

He put the clock on the seat beside him. 'I expect,' he echoed, wondering if he'd bother to cook anything. 'See you in the morning, then. Bye . . .'

'Bye and . . . and Peter . . .' Gillian leaned through the open window, her voice quiet. 'Thanks for being so nice to the old people. They are square, aren't they? Of course they can't help it. I just wish Mum wouldn't try to impress people and Dad goes to the opposite extreme and makes it plain he couldn't care less and . . .'

'And you?' Peter smiled at her. 'Caught in the middle. How d'you feel?'

Gillian hesitated, her youthful face worried as she thought.

'Well, in a way I'm like Dad—I couldn't care less but the truth is, I do care. I always want people to like me, I'm afraid.'

'Why be afraid? What's wrong about that?'

'I'm not sure but . . . but doesn't it also imply a . . . a sense of lack of self-confidence?' she asked earnesly.

'Not necessarily. You like people so you want them to like you. It might imply lack of self-confidence if you hated people and still expected them to like you. You can only expect to receive what you give. You give love so you expect it . . .'

He started the engine and Gillian stood back, waving. How frail and young she looked, he thought, as he drove up the hill to Puffin Cottage. She was a mass of contradictions— like all the Yeltons. Sometimes serious, sometimes gay. Saying such strange things. Yet he had said strange things, too. What on earth had made him say: 'You can only expect to receive what you give?'

What had he to give to people? He always did his best to cure his patients but . . . but he certainly didn't love them. Was that the reason then, that no one loved him?

CHAPTER SIX

As the days passed, Gillian was elated with the success she was having with Peter. Already he seemed less miserable, was getting an outdoor look, no longer felt stiff and his garden was beginning to take shape. Every morning, he exercised Walkabout for her, sometimes they rode over the sands together, the dogs racing round. Nearly every evening they met at a different house. All the same, there was something *odd* about him. He seemed to

56

notice only the superficial things.

Like the visit to the Oswald's to dinner. A super dinner with everything done to impress the new neighbour, but one thing that, to Gillian, stood out a mile. Yet Peter never noticed it for afterwards when they were talking about the Oswalds—he with his bald head and dark beard, Gwen with her shoulder-length blonde hair, rather languid voice and constant quotations from poets—Peter had merely commented:

'You don't usually expect to find intellectuals living in such a wealthy home, somehow. I thought they lived in studios and rather unsavoury quarters.'

'Was that all you noticed?' She had felt vaguely disappointed. 'What about Lyndy?'

'The child? Oh, yes, well—that's quite normal for an only child, isn't it? They invent imaginary friends. I was surprised that the Oswalds were so concerned about it.'

Gillian had sighed. Peter was no better than the rest. They couldn't—or wouldn't see the truth.

'At *ten* years of age, do children talk to imaginary friends?' Gillian had asked. 'Don't you see that child needs someone to love? Someone that needs her. She's terribly lonely. You know the way her parents talk. Those long involved arguments in which you go round in circles and come out where you went in. Lyndy is always out of her depth ...' Gillian had laughed. 'As I was, most of the time, I thought you carried the banner well.'

'I enjoy a good argument. Talking of the child, why don't the Oswalds have another? An only child, as I well know, is always lonely.'

'Gwen refuses. Says one is quite enough of a bind. Yes, she did.'

Gillian had nodded her head energetically as she saw the look on Peter's face. 'They never wanted children—they've always said so. Now they're worried in case Lyndy isn't a genius. They'd see it as a failure on their part if their child isn't as brilliant as they are—or as they think they are.'

'Well, what's the solution?' Peter had asked patiently and that had annoyed her—for she hated it when people spoke like that as if she was just being a difficult child.

'I don't know. I'm just so sorry for Lyndy.'

Then Peter had said a surprising thing. Though, in a way, perhaps it was not so surprising after all, for it was typical of the way he always behaved.

'You're so sorry for people, Gillian. It isn't always a good idea. One day, you could be badly hurt . . .'

She had stared at him, words waiting to flow out to explain that you *had* to care about other people but her mother had come into the room and the conversation had to end.

Now, as she and Brummel painted the stables and tidied things up in preparation for the summer season, she found herself constantly thinking about Peter. There was no doubt he was much better—in health and unhappiness for he had plenty to do.

She chuckled as she dipped the brush into the paint, remembering Peter's first evening at the Judo class. How startled and indignant he had looked when she had thrown him. Effortlessly. But now he was a keen member and—best of all—little Ginger was no longer getting so teased about his name. Peter had helped him, there. That was a big thing.

Solak came to nuzzle up against her. 'In a moment,' she promised. The sun was streaming down and Spring, though late this year, was really in the air. 'I know it's time for your walk, love, but I must finish this . . .'

'Can I help?' a deep familiar voice said.

Gillian turned hastily. 'Oh, Peter, how nice of you but what about your work?'

As usual the tips of his ears went bright red, just like her Dad's and Peter looked uncomfortable.

'I've got some thinking to do and . . . well, I find physical work often helps.'

'Good . . .' She found him a paint brush and a tin, lent him an overall and watched him roll up his sleeves. 'As soon as this bit is finished, I've got to take the dogs for a run. The tide'll be out so I thought the sands . . .'

Peter grinned. 'Suits me fine.'

As they painted, Gillian kept glancing at

him. How he had changed, she kept thinking. Now he was whistling softly.

'It's not so bad after all, is it?' she asked and then wished she hadn't as Peter turned to look at her questioningly. 'I mean living here. You hated it at first.'

Peter laughed. He had put on some weight, she noticed.

'I had nothing to do—that's why I hated it. Now I'm so busy I haven't time to be bored.'

She was worried. 'Peter, I . . . look,' she tried to find the right words. 'Peter, we're not stopping you from your writing, are we? I did tell everyone you weren't to be asked out in the daytime as that was your working time. You're sure we're not?'

He laughed. 'Sure you're not. As a matter of fact, you were right. There's enough material here to write several books.'

She smiled joyfully, unaware of the sudden startling beauty the happiness gave her, wondering a little at the odd way Peter stared at her and then looked away hastily.

'I must say you have some queer characters . . .' he went on but, somehow, his voice had changed. It sounded impersonal, no longer so relaxed and friendly. 'Maybe it's the sea air. I've nearly finished.'

'Good.' She wondered what she had said or what had happened to make him change. Had she unwittingly said something to offend him?

Almost silently they later walked along the

sands, the dogs racing round them excitedly. They went round the cove to the caravan world and Peter told her of his first sight of it.

'I was appalled and so thankful I was on the other side. Then I felt rather mean as, after all, it is their holiday. What right have I to resent them being there?'

She laughed. 'I wish some of our neighbours felt like you. The summer is one long moan of complaints.'

'Do they come over to us much?'

'Not much. Least, I don't think so and they rarely come into this cove. The tide goes out a long way but races in at a frightening rate. Very easy to get drowned there. They put up warning notices but you know what people are like.'

'It can never happen to them,' he said dryly.

Gillian laughed. 'You're so right. Look, Peter, if we go inland down here there's a wonderful little valley at the back. When I was younger I collected all the wild flowers there I could find and stuck them in a book. I got over a hundred different flowers. Like to see it— the valley, I mean?'

'Of course.'

They walked inland over the concrete paths laid down near the still empty caravans and round the lower part of the cliff. Here was a small valley half hidden by huge overhanging rocks and with trees packed closely together as if to keep out intruders.

The trees were covered with fresh green leaves, spangled with small white flowers. There were violets and cowslips and a few early bluebells. Birds were singing as Peter and Gillian walked slowly along the narrow path, single file, the dogs ahead one moment, the next distracted by an exciting scent. Solak was burrowing in the ground until Gillian called him then he came racing, his lovely long silk coat glistening.

The wood ended just behind the Yelton's house.

'Care for a cuppa?' she asked casually and then caught hold of his arm. 'Peter, would you like to do your Boy Scout's good deed for the day?'

He looked amused. 'I thought I'd done it.'

'That was to help me—this is to help Fiona.'

'Fiona? Have I met her?'

Gillian shook her head. 'No for she can never go out. Look, just half an hour and you'll make Fiona and her mother so happy, Peter . . .'

'All right.'

Gillian beamed. 'Bless you. Just let me shut up the dogs for Mrs. Morris gets an allergy if dogs go near her . . .' She saw his amused smile and she laughed. 'At least she says so.'

She came back in a moment, looking down at her paint-smeared jeans and white shirt, flapping in the sea breeze. 'One thing the old lady is half blind, poor darling, otherwise she might be shocked. Just to hear a new voice acts as a tonic for her. This way.'

The cottage was on the first track that went across the cliff. A pretty little cottage with pink curtains and a matching front door. A wisp of blue smoke drifted out of the chimney. There were pink geraniums in the window boxes and some late daffodils in the garden.

The door was opened by a tall thin girl with jet black hair brushed straight back, and dark unhappy eyes. Her face lightened as she saw Gillian.

'So you made it, Gillian. How nice of you. Do come in. Mother was saying the other day she'd like to see you. She just forgets time, you know. I mean you were here two days ago yet to hear her, it was . . .'

'Two months. I know.' Gillian laughed. 'Look, Fiona—this is Peter Richardson. He's taken the Trents' cottage for six months. Peter—this is Fiona.'

Fiona glanced quickly at the tall thin man by Gillian's side and turned back to Gillian.

'Could you stay half an hour? That'll give me time and . . .' she said eagerly.

'That's what we came for, Fiona. Look, make it three quarters of an hour only you'd better be around just before we go or your mother will think.'

Fiona nodded. 'You're right. Tea's ready. I've put an extra cup and saucer for Mr. Richardson.'

Peter glanced at Gillian who smiled at him innocently so he said nothing but merely followed the two girls into the dark front room of the cottage.

'Mother,' Fiona said cheerfully, 'you've got two visitors . . .'

A plump woman sitting in a chair by the window moved restlessly. 'A pleasant change to have a visitor. Fiona, these pillows are most uncomfortable. I'd have thought by now you'd know how to . . .'

'I'm sorry, Mother . . .' Fiona fussed round the chair, altering the cushions, trying to make her mother comfortable and failing.

'Oh dear, my poor back. Well, I suppose I'll have to put up with it. Who are my visitors, Fiona? You might at least introduce them.'

Fiona's face was red as she apologized. 'This is Gillian and . . . Mr. Richardson.'

'Ah, Mr. Richardson . . .' Mrs. Norris's plump face changed, became alight with interest as she held out her hand. 'How nice of you to waste your time calling on an old lady. I've heard so much about you, Mr. Richardson. Gillian tells me you're writing a book. Who is it about?'

She turned towards Fiona. 'Don't just stand there, girl, make us some tea. Do sit down, Mr. Richardson, I've always felt sure that my life would make a wonderful book only I have no idea of how to write it. Do tell me how you start writing and how d'you work it all out. I think it is very clever of you . . .'

Gillian found it hard to hide her smile as she saw Peter's bright red ears so she escaped to the kitchen to help Fiona and speed her on her way.

'What d'you think of Peter?' Gillian asked as she carefully heated the teapot.

'Peter? Oh, Mr. Richardson. He looks all right . . .' Fiona said as she hastily took off her apron and straightened her pink suit. 'I must fly, Gillian. Bless you, love . . .' She kissed her lightly and ran out of the cottage.

Gillian carefully carried the tray into the front room, disliking as usual the heavy walnut furniture that made the room seem smaller than it already was. Peter was sitting, leaning forward, talking plainly for the old lady to hear what he said, though she was doing most of the talking. As Gillian poured out the tea, carefully putting Mrs. Norris's cup on the table by her side, she tried not to smile as she heard the incessant flow of words.

'Well, my dear boy, of course I was young and had many wealthy young men after me but I married for love and I never really regretted it. We had a hard life. I could tell you things that went on in Sarawak that would turn your hair white. I just wish I could write it all down. It would make most interesting reading . . .'

Gillian sat quietly for she was obviously redundant. Peter was a new voice, a new pair of ears, and Mrs. Norris was making the most of it. Every now and then, Gillian glanced anxiously at the clock, prepared to leap into the conversation if there was a pause. Anything rather than give Mrs. Norris a chance to ask where Fiona was! At last there was the sound of the back door closing and in a moment Fiona noiselessly crept into the room. Her cheeks were flushed and her eyes sparkling as she smiled at Gillian and nodded in answer to the question in Gillian's eyes.

After a few moments, Gillian said she was sorry but they must go. Mrs. Norris looked as if she was going to cry as she clung to Peter's hand.

'This has been the happiest afternoon I've had for months,' she said. 'Please do come again. I'm a prisoner here and life gets very dull and boring. No one to talk to, intelligent that is . . .' she added, giving a dour look in the direction of Fiona. 'Do clear away the tea things, Fiona. They look so untidy there. Well, I suppose if you've got to go, I can't keep you but please do come again, Mr. Richardson,' she said eagerly. 'We are attune—we talk the same language. Such a treat to meet a man like you . . .'

Finally Gillian managed to get Peter out of the cottage. Walking down the hill, Peter asked:

'What's wrong with her?'

'I'm not sure. She's been a semi-invalid for years. Sometimes it's her back, sometimes her kidneys, or her feet—there's always something.'

'I don't think there's anything wrong with her at all. Her daughter probably fusses too much.'

Gillian stared at him. 'Fiona fusses? I like that! Her mother demands instant and constant attention. You heard the way she spoke to Fiona.'

'Why did Fiona vanish?'

They were strolling towards Gillian's house now. 'To meet her boy friend. I always let her know when I'm going in . . .'

'Only today it was *we*,' Peter pointed out, looking at her. 'How could you be sure I'd agree?'

'I knew you would. You've got a kind nature.' Gillian said, looking at him quickly and fluttering her eyelashes. He tried not to smile. He'd noticed recently that she always did that when she was not sure if she was saying the right thing.

'Me—a kind nature? I'd like you to hear what some of my friends think of me. You're the only person who's ever called me kind.'

'Oh you're not always kind,' Gillian told him. 'But you're never *unkind*. At least, not on purpose. You're thoughtless, that's all.'

He was startled. 'Thoughtless? Now what have I done?'

'You haven't done anything. That's just it. You take the line of least resistance, shelter

67

behind your impersonal manner to avoid getting involved. You're terrified of becoming fond of anyone in case you'll get hurt. Isn't that right?' Gillian looked up at him, almost defiantly, and then he saw her flutter her eyelashes. 'Aren't I right?'

'I don't think so,' he said slowly. 'I admit I don't want to get married but that's because ...' he stopped abruptly, and then began again: 'My work is the kind that ... well, bluntly, I can work better alone.'

'I'm beginning to think you're a James Bond,' Gillian teased. 'Everything is so mysterious. I can't see that if you really loved someone it need affect your work. I thought you might be a doctor but then I changed my mind.'

He frowned. 'Now what made you change your mind?'

She waved her hands vaguely. 'Because you have no compassion or understanding for anyone. Take Fiona, I see her as a martyr, a virtual prisoner because of her mother's possessive love, unable to marry the man she loves because she's afraid her mother will have a fit or be terribly ill and Fiona's the type who would never forgive herself, but I'm sure you don't see Fiona like that. Now do you?'

He looked at her. 'Frankly no. You usually find that type of daughter delights in being a martyr. People admire her, feel sorry for her, she feels important because her mother needs

68

her. No, she enjoys that sort of life. If she didn't, she'd do something constructive about it.'

'And what—' Gillian asked sarcastically, 'do you mean by constructive?'

'If I believed my mother was making it all up, I'd insist on her seeing a specialist. If I didn't want to devote my life to her, I'd get her in a hospital or home.'

'You make it sound so simple ...' Gillian had her hand on the gate of her house. A dog barked in the background. A cockerel crowed. 'You seem to have overlooked one important point, Peter. Fiona loves her mother. But then, of course, you can't be expected to understand for you just don't know what love is.'

CHAPTER SEVEN

As the days became weeks, Peter was surprised one morning when he had gone outside the cottage, to see just how beautiful Cornwall was. Somehow he hadn't noticed it before. Maybe it was because the sun was warm and shining, turning the vast expanse of sea into sparkling silver.

Maybe because he had learned to adapt himself to this new life or could it be because he had *looked* at the scenery for the first time?

The coast line was superb with its deep

coves, huge beaches and rocks against which the sea furiously flung itself. He noticed that the cottage above his had an inmate. Normally empty, looking drab, today the front door was open with pop music pouring out of it.

Peter didn't disapprove of pop music but neither was he a fan of it and he felt annoyed because the music was so loud. He wondered who on earth had taken the cottage and for how long?

As he hurried down the hill for his morning exercise of Walkabout, he realized how much he owed his present state of resigned contentment to Gillian Yelton. At times, she made him so angry that he found it hard not to tell her so but then she would look at him with that innocent smile and flutter her eye lashes and he hadn't the heart to scold her. He knew she meant well, that she was trying to help him, but he didn't need anyone's help and that was the truth.

All the same, despite Gillian's irritating habit of involving him in situations he'd have preferred to avoid, at the same time it was Gillian who had introduced him to the local people, Gillian who had shown him how to fill the long empty days with constructive work, Gillian who had made him laugh and who looked so ridiculously young and frail.

He had come to know most of the local people and, as Gillian had said once, they were a queer lot. Take Petra and Ethel Thomas, the two elderly sisters who lived alone together. On the surface they were a devoted couple, Petra the dominant one, Ethel meekly but happily doing what she was told. Yet when you dined there you felt the undercurrent of resentment and hatred. Even he, cold blooded and blind to the truth of things as Gillian had once said, could feel the emnity between the two sisters.

Then there was the widow, Bridget. So young and pretty, only twenty-six, with a child of nine. Bridget worked in Cudjack so Mike, the boy, was often on his own and could be seen sitting miserably on the doorstep, waiting for his mother to come home. Since his father's death, Mike—according to Bessie Beaky, the village schoolmistress—had changed completely, though he worked infinitely harder at school, he refused to play with the other children and would escape home as soon as he could.

Then there was Jacquie Box and the family of children, Ginger being one of them. Jacquie was a lovely girl of eighteen with enormous expressive eyes, a sweetly happy smile, and long slim legs. Gillian was sorry for Jacquie but Peter had decided Jacquie enjoyed being the mother of the family. Her father, in the early fifties, was an outstandingly handsome and amusing man with only slightly greying hair. He had been friendly to Peter, as indeed they all were. Yet according to Gillian, there was a strain in the household. Jacquie's father had 'changed' since his wife died, Gillian said. He was rarely at home and took little notice of the children, leaving everything to Jacquie.

The Kerrs were another odd family. Obviously wealthy, they had a beautiful house near the huge school. Elderly parents for the seventeen year old daughter, they were very possessive and according to Gillian, it was almost impossible for Prue, their daughter, to have any social life at all.

'It's so stupid of them,' Gillian had said angrily. 'Can't they see that we've got to be independent and allowed to stand on our own feet? Don't they realize that the way to lose your child is to cling to her?'

Peter had said his impression was that they loved Prue very much and Gillian had almost snapped at him:

'A funny kind of love, I call it, but then what d'you know of love?' she had asked and walked out of the room angrily.

Now as he reached the Yelton's house, Peter was thinking of how often Gillian had accused him of being incapable of understanding what love meant. Well, what did it mean, he wondered. Maybe he should ask her . . .

Even as he thought this, she came running round the house, 'Oh Peter . . .' she said breathlessly. 'Poor Walkabout isn't very fit. Dad's having a look at him now. Will you have one of the other horses?'

'I don't mind . . . Gillian, I want to ask you something . . .' he caught hold of her arm, swinging her gently to face him.

He saw the surprise in her slanting eyes, followed by wariness. 'What about?' she asked quickly.

'Love.'

He saw her quick frown and then, as it vanished, to be followed by a smile, she laughed. 'You're kidding. You're not interested in love. You've always said so.'

'Have I . . .' he paused as a cuckoo called. He looked up. Everyone had said how late the cuckoos were. It was years since he'd heard one. 'I was wondering what you mean by love.'

'What I . . . what *I* mean by love?'

He nodded. 'Yes, you. I can't help feeling you bandy the word around and yet you don't really know what it does mean.'

'Do you?'

The dogs came racing, jumping up at Peter, whom they had accepted, and quietened by Gillian's quiet voice.

'No I don't,' Peter said bluntly. 'That's why I'm asking you.' He let go of her arm and she clasped her hands together, looking down at them.

'Well, there are all kinds of love,' she began.

'There's only one word: love. That's the word I want explained.'

'Well . . .' she spoke very slowly, her eyes half-closed as if she was looking for the right words. 'The way I see *love* is when you want to make someone happy.'

'At that rate,' his voice was slightly sarcastic, 'you love the whole of mankind. I'm talking of individual love. What would you require of a man before you loved him?'

Gillian's eyes opened in a flash—he saw the surprise on her face. 'Nothing.'

'Oh come, Gillian, you're not as dumb as that. You must know what you expect of your Prince Charming.'

'Of course I don't ... How can I? When I meet him, I'll just love him. I shan't know why. I just will.'

'You mean it could be anyone?' Peter said.

She nodded. 'But it would be the right one.'

'How would you know?'

'Ah ...' she looked a bit frightened. 'That's it, Peter, how do you know. I've often wondered. Does it suddenly hit you or is love something that slowly ripens, a sort of friendship becoming more than friendship. What d'you think?'

He shrugged. 'I'm no expert.'

'But you must have been in love sometime?' Gillian said earnestly.

Frowning, Peter looked back into his past. 'I suppose so but they were mere crushes. You know, sort of momentary infatuations. I'd meet a girl and think she was *it* and then, a few weeks later, she wasn't *it* and I ...'

'Just dropped her?'

Peter grinned. 'Yes—but often she dropped me. We'd both woken up to the truth. I don't call that love.'

'Nor do I.'

'Look, Gillian, what sort of man d'you want to marry? You must have some idea.'

Gillian screwed up her eyes again and was obviously thinking hard. Then she opened her eyes and smiled.

'I just don't know, Peter. I want him to be fond of dogs and of children. I want him to like dancing and swimming. I want him to be kind . . .'

'He sounds rather a bore . . .' Peter teased.

'Oh honestly . . .' Gillian sounded exasperated and turned away, 'I might have guessed. You were only joking.' She moved fast towards the stables and he had to run to catch up.

'I wasn't, Gillian,' he told her, 'truth, I wasn't. I wondered what you meant by the word *love*.'

She gave him a strange look. 'And d'you know now?'

'Miss Gillian . . . happen we was to . . .' Old Brummel came hurrying out of one of the stables and the conversation ceased.

Peter rode the horse Gillian gave him and they raced across the sand. Afterwards she asked him to breakfast. This happened every day and was so normal that Alice, the Nanny, always had his favourite eggs, sausages and bacon ready. Sometimes he said he oughtn't to take advantage of their generosity and Gillian would point out that she was the one in debt to him for exercising the horse.

'Of course when the season opens,' she said that morning after his usual routine apology, 'the horses will be booked up. I teach at the school as well as visitors. I get very busy.'

'You enjoy it?'

She smiled at him. 'Of course. That's why I do it. I love a job that keeps me in the open air. Don't you?'

'I don't get the chance in my job,' he began and saw the questions in her eyes so hastily he spoke of the first thing he could think of because, so far, he had managed to keep it secret that he was a doctor. 'By the way, the cottage above mine is occupied. I don't know who the tenant is but the most ghastly music was blaring out this morning.'

Gillian's face lit up. 'That must be Dirk Thatcher. Oh, I'm so glad.'

'Well, I am not!' Nanny said as she gave them some fresh hot milk for another cup of coffee. 'I never did approve of that young man and you know it well, Gillian.'

'Oh, Nanny,' Gillian was laughing. 'Does it matter that he wears his hair long?'

'He could at least wash it,' the elderly woman said testily. 'And his ghastly clothes, no manners, neither. I don't know what you see in him.'

'A boy friend of yours?' Peter asked, glancing at Gillian and watched the pale rose colour slowly flood her cheeks.

'He comes down every summer—at the week-ends only. He's an artist. Quite good but nothing he paints ever sells. He reckons he's too good . . .'

In the background Nanny snorted a little and Gillian had to smile. She looked at Peter, then at Nanny's back, shrugged her shoulders and lifted her eyebrows.

'We're organizing a bazaar for the church, Peter, and we're doing a lot of painting for it. I wondered if you'd help me for some of the stalls are big. We thought we'd make it very contemporary with dazzling colours, you know. If you can spare a couple of hours this afternoon—say round about four—I'd be most grateful.'

Peter stared at her. He wondered if that ridiculous gifts of hers of reading his thoughts had told her that four o'clock was his *bad time*. His lonely, aimless time when there seemed nothing to do.

'Sure . . .' He kept his voice casual. 'I'll be taking a break about then. Where shall I meet you?'

'I'll come along and pick you up, shall I?' Gillian suggested as they finished their breakfast. 'You haven't been to our church yet.'

He looked at her quickly and saw that her

77

words were not meant as a rebuke but as a statement.

'We've got a new Vicar and he's very green, poor chap,' Gillian went on. 'Just doesn't know how to handle the locals. His wife, too, tries terribly hard but it takes a long time here to get accepted. Most of us are sorry for them and we want this, their first Church bazaar, to be a success.'

Most of us, Gillian had said, Peter thought and wondered how many people could be included in those three words *most of us*. He had a strong feeling that Gillian was the only person. He'd never met anyone in his life before who bent over so far backwards to help others. Surely it was up to the Vicar and his wife . . .

'All right,' he said, 'I'll expect you.'

He walked back up the side of the cliff to Puffin Cottage, looking at the morning ahead and wondering what to do with himself. A couple of hours of gardening perhaps, for the sun was shining without being too hot and the pathetic patch was certainly beginning to look better. Then, perhaps a walk? And this afternoon? Until four? The hours seemed to stretch away ahead of him.

Maybe he'd stroll down towards the Raines' cottage and talk to Mike, who would be sitting on the doorstep, patiently waiting for his mother. It wasn't right that a boy of that age should be at home alone nor was it right that attractive young Bridget, his widowed mother, should have to work.

Peter sighed, took off his coat and rolled up his shirt sleeves. Even his washing problems had been solved by Gillian. The Yeltons had a large washing machine and 'Nanny' loved washing, Gillian had said and added with a smile:

'She's a terrible saver and if you gave her something each week for doing your washing, it would be a great help to her. She's alone in the world, but for us. She was Mum's Nanny too, you see, and she's always thinking of her "old age". It would be a kindness to her.'

So it worked out very well. And all thanks, again, to Gillian, Peter thought, as he began to sort out the fresh lot of small plants Philip Yelton had sent up to him. Peter liked Philip and wished heartily he'd never thought up the stupid lie of being a writer and that he could tell the truth that he was a doctor for there was so much they could discuss that would interest them both. Still, David Rugg was right, Peter thought with a sigh. They had a good doctor for the neighbourhood but he was grossly overworked and Peter felt sure that the local suburbans, as he liked to call them, would turn to him for advice and help if they knew the truth. After all, he ate at their houses and enjoyed their friendliness so he could hardly have refused them help.

'Hey ...' a deep voice interrupted him.

79

'Who the hell are you?'

Peter straightened his back slowly and turned and found himself facing a short thin lad with rumpled blond hair that rested on his shoulders, sideboards and the beginnings of a beard. He was wearing a purple shirt and yellow slacks. Now he was leaning on the white wicket gate, grinning at Peter.

'What's a man like you doing at a place like this?'

Peter frowned. None of your business, he felt like snapping and then remembered that this was Gillian's 'boy friend'.

'You must be Dirk Thatcher, the artist,' he said, keeping his voice friendly.

Dirk grinned. 'Ah—do I sniff the scent of Gillian? Has she been talking about me?'

'Simply that you were a good but unrecognized artist and that you came down every week-end in the summer.'

'That's right. And you?'

'I'm Peter Richardson, a . . .' Peter's tongue stopped just in time and he went on more slowly; 'I'm here for six months to . . .'

Dirk lifted a hand. 'Hey, hold it, dad. I think I can guess. You're a cloak and dagger guy. Right? You've been sent here to spy on the locals and see who's doing the smuggling.'

'Smuggling?' Peter was startled.

Dirk grinned. 'Sure, of course there's some smuggling, man. This the Cornish coast and all! So you're not here for that. Wait . . . you're

80

a Civil Servant and have come down to catch the income tax evaders. Right?'

Peter laughed. 'Wrong, again. I'm probably one of the biggest evaders myself. No, you're way out, Mr. Thatcher.'

'Hey, steady on, what's your drag? Call me Dirk—Peter. You know, I have a feeling our little Gillian has taken you under her wing.' Dirk was grinning again. 'She's got so many lame ducks to love that I sometimes wonder she finds time to breathe. Am I right?'

'She's been extremely kind and helpful . . .'

Dirk shouted with laughter. 'I can imagine. She does that to me. Wallows in kindness. One of these days, she's going to have a shock. I'm always telling her to quit it.'

'Quit it?'

Dirk nodded his head violently so that his hair swung. 'Yes, quit all this do-good business. People don't appreciate it and she'll get hurt.'

It was precisely what Peter had thought but he found himself defending Gillian.

'It's part of her make up. She doesn't do it consciously, you know. She just does it without thought.'

Dirk nodded. 'She certainly digs it, man. Waste of energy, I guess. She'd be better off if she concentrated on herself and led a sensible life.'

Peter smiled. 'That's what I told her. She was rather annoyed when I said she was wasting her life.'

Dirk nodded again. 'She would be. She's happy—just making others happy. A funny sort of kid but ...' his eyes narrowed as he looked at Peter. 'If she gets hurt ...' he said, his voice low and suddenly threatening. 'D'you chat her up?'

'Chat her up?' Peter repeated, momentarily puzzled and suddenly understanding and he felt heat in his face and hoped he had not turned red. 'Heavens above, Dirk, look at me. I'm thirty-five and Gillian is just a kid. She sees me as an uncle.'

'Good,' Dirk grinned, his emnity vanished. 'It's not that I find her groovy but she's a good kid and I wouldn't want her hurt. I guess you're right, though. You're much too old ... Well, I'm going down to say Hi to Nanny and make her mad.' He chuckled. 'I really get a kick out of her disapproving frown with poor little Gillian running in circles to keep sensitive me from being hurt. See you ...' He gave an airy wave of his hand and made his way down the hill.

Peter, stood leaning on the spade, watching Dirk. He was slightly bow-legged and walked a bit clumsily. He stuck his head out aggressively. That dreadful hair! Yet there was something odd about Dirk. Something that didn't ring true. As Peter went back to work, he made up his mind to ask Gillian a few questions about his new neighbour.

It was just gone three when he heard the car

draw up. Peter was on his hands and knees, digging small holes in the friable soil and gently planting each little plant as Gillian had showed him.

'Peter . . . what on earth . . .' A silvery rather attractive female voice startled him.

He turned so suddenly that he lost balance and sat on the ground, luckily not on the newly planted seedlings. He stared, amazed, at the tall elegant girl getting out of a white Jaguar. Lucille Harding!

'What d'you think you're doing?' she asked him as she opened the white wicket gate and walked towards him, an amazing picture against the background of blue, sun-washed sea and the new yellow gorse that was colouring the hillside.

Her long blonde hair was elaborately waved high on her head. She wore a pale blue silk suit. She walked unevenly on high heels, holding a white handbag in one hand. And wearing long white gloves!

Perhaps it was the last that set him off for he suddenly wanted to laugh. If Lucille knew how funny she looked! He overcame his mirth and stood up, brushing the mud off him and looking at his dirty hands.

'Gardening,' he answered her question briefly. 'I might ask what are you doing?'

She smiled sweetly. 'I came to see you. I missed you,' she added wistfully.

He led the way into the cottage. 'Just sit

down. I'll wash my hands and then what about a cup of coffee?'

'Have you got a maid or a manservant?' she asked, her voice amused, looking round her with scorn before sitting down. 'Don't tell me you can make coffee.'

'I most certainly can,' he said. He'd known her for nearly ten years and was well used to her charm. 'I can even boil an egg and fry a chop.'

'You must be out of your mind . . .' Lucille was pulling off her gloves with slowly deliberate movements. her eyes narrowed as she smiled at him. 'Wasting your time like this.'

'I won't be a moment.' He escaped to the tiny bathroom, then hastily went into his bedroom and changed into a clean white shirt and cream terylene slacks before going back.

'The sun's nice,' he said. 'How about sitting outside.'

Lucille's hand went to her face. 'Heavens above, no. You know how delicate my skin is. Now do sit down and tell me what this is all about, Peter. Suddenly you vanish without a word to anyone. You can imagine how everyone talked.'

Peter poured himself a whisky, asked her if she'd like one but Lucille shook her head.

'Peter, I asked you a question.'

'How did you find out where I was?'

She smiled. 'I have my ways. I bullied David without success so . . . one day I saw a letter lying on the hall table addressed to you. Simple as that. A little ingenuity.'

'Didn't David tell you I wanted to be left alone?'

Lucille smiled. 'Of course but I knew that wouldn't apply to me, Peter. I mean, we're more than friends. Aren't we?'

There was a little silence as he studied her face. He could never understand why Lucille chased him. Maybe because he always ran away. She was a born hunter and found a prey who escaped her constantly exciting. Maybe if he said he worshipped the ground she walked on, she'd lose all interest and leave him alone. Sometimes he was tempted but there was always the chance that she might believe him and fall into his arms ... No, he thought, his mouth unconsciously smiling, she'd pull him into her arms! Lucille had to be the dominant one.

'Well.' She sounded annoyed. 'Why are you laughing?'

He looked at the coloured liquid in his glass. 'No reason.' All of a sudden he felt tired. 'I'm here because of my health, Lucille. That's all there was to it. I knew I was overdoing things but when I began having black-outs, David told me it was time I took a rest. That's why I'm here.'

Lucille leaned forward eagerly. 'But it's all so ridiculous. You could have had a holiday, surely. Spain, or even Greece. Somewhere

85

interesting. Why choose a dump like this?'

Peter laughed. 'That's what I thought it was at first but it grows on you in time.'

Her face changed. 'You're not serious, Peter? I mean, you wouldn't want to give up your work in London and settle down here?'

He laughed again. 'I can't imagine it but I find it very pleasant for a change.'

'But what do you *do*?' Lucille demanded. 'It must be absolute purgatory for you. Doing nothing.'

He looked at her ruefully. 'I hardly do nothing. I ride every morning for an hour. I garden. I visit local people who are my friends. I go out to dinner most nights.'

Lucille sat up abruptly, her back like a poker, her beautiful face disdainful. 'And you call that doing something. How can you, Peter? Look, you're just crazy to be here. Come back and slacken off a bit. You're— look, Peter, there's no need for you to work so hard but if you were in London, well, at least we could go out together and . . .'

'That would be a change.'

She suddenly glared. 'Well, it never was my fault we went out so seldom. You're . . . I don't know how to say it, but you are too ridiculously dedicated to your work. All work and no play . . .'

'Makes Peter a better doctor,' Peter said, jumping up and refilling his glass. 'Look, let's drop it, Lucille. I agreed with David to come here and relax for six months. I'm his partner and owe it to him to stay well . . .'

'I don't think there's anything wrong with you. David has some ulterior motive. He wanted you out of the way . . .' she said, her voice triumphant. 'I bet he's got some scheme up his sleeve.'

'There is nothing wrong with me,' Peter told her slowly, feeling his temper rising. 'I overworked and need a good rest. That's all. I could have taken a month's leave and have gone back to plunge into the mad whirl again and had another blackout. Six months gives me time to relax properly and . . . well, get ready for a fresh start.'

'You think this sort of . . . well, cabbage existence is doing you good?' Lucille asked.

Peter went to the window. He thought he had heard a car. He turned round to face Lucille.

'Yes, I do think it's doing me good. I'm beginning to see people, Lucille. See them as people and not as patients. I'm beginning to understand something of their personal troubles, not merely their physical symptoms.'

'Oh, Peter, for crying out loud,' Lucille's voice was impatient. 'Stop being so corny. You're not planning to do psychiatry, are you?'

She stood up and moved to his side, her hand on his. She moved a little closer so that the perfume she wore made his nostrils tingle. She looked up at him, her eyes soft and imploring.

'You forgot about me, Peter. How I'd miss you. Life isn't the same without you there . . .'

He moved away with a jerk. 'Nonsense, Lucille, you have plenty of friends apart from your devotion to your work.'

'My work . . .' she said scornfully. 'You know why I became a doctor, Peter. Simply so that we—you and I—could talk the same language.'

'That's absurd,' he began and stopped, instead he stared at her. She was looking up at him, her face grave and sincere. It frightened him for a moment. Surely it wasn't the truth? She couldn't love him as much as that.

'It's not absurd, Peter. I mean it.'

She picked up her gloves and began to pull them on slowly, then turned to look at him as he stood by the open window.

'I mean it, Peter. I love you and I intend to be, one day, Mrs. Richardson. I know that you love me but you are so scared of personal entanglements that you run a hundred miles when you hear the word *love*. One day, you'll change your mind. You'll find you'll need someone to love you and I'll be waiting.'

She opened the front door and smiled sweetly at him, a sweetness he knew hid her frustration for she was not a good loser.

'Well, I'll pop down now and then to make sure you don't forget me . . .' She stopped as a car drew up outside the gate. He turned and saw Gillian get out of the car and come running.

'Who on earth is that?' Lucille demanded.

Gillian had seen them. She faltered and half-stopped and then came on. She was wearing paint-smeared green jeans and a yellow blouse. Her short dark hair was wind-blown, her cheeks red, her nose shiny and she had forgotten to use make-up. The contrast between her fresh natural beauty and Lucille's older contrived loveliness struck Peter at once. They were opposites. Completely different in appearance and in character.

'Hi Gillian,' he said calmly. 'I'd like you to meet my old friend, Lucille Harding. Lucille, this is Gillian Yelton. She lets me ride her horses.'

Gillian smiled politely. She looked for once, at a loss. 'Peter, had you forgotten . . .'

'Of course not. Lucille is just leaving.' He looked down at his clothes. 'You go on ahead, Gillian, I'll see Lucille off and then change into some suitable clothes. I drive faster than you so I'll soon catch you up.'

Gillian smiled. 'As you say, Peter. See you just now.' She smiled politely at Lucille and then ran back down the path to her car.

'And who,' Lucille asked coldly, 'is that and what does she do?'

Peter began to walk down the garden path, leaving Lucille with no alternative but to follow him as he talked over his shoulder.

'Gillian's father is the local vet her mother is Head Librarian. Gillian runs a very flourishing riding school in the summer and in the winter, does odd jobs.'

'A layabout . . .' Lucille's voice was scornful. 'How old is she? Fifteen? Shouldn't she be still at school or did they throw her out?'

Peter was startled at the quick anger that surged through him. Why, Gillian was worth a dozen Lucilles. Maybe a hundred.

'She is twenty,' he said gravely, 'and knows what she is doing. She gives the local people a lot of happiness.'

'And you?' Lucille's voice rose in anger as he opened the door of her car. 'Does she give you a lot of happiness?'

Peter smiled at her and slammed the door shut as she settled herself behind the wheel.

'Yes, Lucille, now I come to think of it, she does,' he said and stood back, watching with amusement, her anger as she shot up the track.

CHAPTER EIGHT

Gillian drove ahead slowly to allow Peter time to say goodbye to his visitor, change into suitable clothes and follow her. The Vicarage was an old-fashioned stone house, hidden away some distance from the church, and the church hall was next door so she wanted him to be able to follow her.

Of course it all depended on how long it took him to say goodbye to his visitor!

Unconsciously Gillian's hands tightened on the steering wheel. It was not normal for her to feel jealous but she could not forget the elegance of the girl, standing so possessively by Peter's side—or the complete beauty of her. Somehow, Gillian thought, she had never pictured Peter with a girl, and yet, oddly enough, having seen him with—what was her name? Oh, yes, Lucille. Having seen him with Lucille, Gillian realized that the beautiful elegant girl was just right for Peter. A girl in her late twenties, mature, sophisticated, beautiful—a girl he had obviously known for a long time.

Gillian drove over the stone bridge across the river, glancing into her mirror but she still couldn't see Peter's car. He knew the way roughly so she decided to park the car by the side of the road just up the hill. There she could watch until she saw him coming and then lead the way.

Sitting there with the lovely trees turning the road into a green avenue, Gillian thought of Peter and Lucille. Was she the reason for Peter's coming to Puffin Cottage? Was Lucille the girl he loved so much he was afraid of love? Perhaps Lucille was married?'

She glanced at her watch and frowned a little. She had promised to be there at a certain time and she hated to keep people waiting. She looked down at her paint-smeared jeans and realized that for the first time in her memory she had felt self-conscious of her clothes. As Lucille had stared at her with those amused, scornful eyes, Gillian had been aware of the sight she must have looked.

That was absurd, she told herself severely. You could hardly wear a silk suit if you were painting in the Church Hall! Glancing in the mirror, she recognized Peter's car coming along the road. With a sigh of relief, she switched on the engine and slid ahead. He hooted in recognition and she led the way.

There were three cars already parked outside the bleak-looking, barn-like Church hall and Peter and Gillian parked side by side.

He smiled as he joined her. He was wearing shorts and an open necked shirt. Both looked expensive.

Gillian was worried. 'You'll get paint all over you . . .'

He laughed. 'I expect so but these are my working clothes so it won't matter. Poor Nanny will curse me, though, so I'll be very careful.'

The vicarage was a small stone house with the windows shining in the sunlight, the cream-coloured curtains hanging neatly. There was the sound of a baby crying.

As Gillian led the way, she glanced up at Peter.

'I hope . . . I hope my turning up like that

didn't hurry your visitor away.'

His lean face relaxed in a smile. 'It helped. I thought she'd never go.'

Gillian failed to hide her surprise. 'You wanted her to go?'

'Of course. She can be awfully boring.'

Catching her breath, Gillian sought for the right words. 'I thought she was very . . . very beautiful.'

'Oh yes, she is, lovely long legs. Good body. Beautiful in fact,' Peter said nonchalantly.

'You've known her for a long time?'

'Goodness yes.' Peter screwed up his eyes as he thought. 'Must be eleven or twelve years. She's in my age group though she doesn't look it.'

There was no chance to talk to Peter alone any more for, as they went into the lofty Hall, Gillian was greeted eagerly.

'You're late . . .' Dirk Thatcher said accusingly as he flourished a paint brush.

'My fault,' Peter told him. 'I had a visitor to get rid of and Gillian had to show me the way . . .'

He knew everyone there. Jacquie Box with several of her brothers and sisters. Young Mike Raines with his detached withdrawn look as he painstakingly painted some boards a vivid orange. Bessie, the school mistress and Sean Jones, the Vicar. Soon Peter was busily painting. It was amazing the knack Gillian had, not only of organizing things but of imbuing other people with her energy and zeal, he thought, for even that extraordinary Dirk Thatcher was working hard!

Through the voices and laughter as they all painted or put together the stalls round the Hall, every now and then Peter could hear Dirk Thatcher's voice. A strange one for it didn't ring true. Almost as if Dirk was acting a part. Still, he and Gillian seemed to have plenty to say to one another, Pctcr thought, casually turning to get more paint and glancing at them. Dirk was laughing, moving his hands about as he spoke, and Gillian was staring at him, a puzzled look on her face.

Peter would have been even more curious had he heard what Dirk was saying:

'What's all the secrecy about? I don't dig it, Gill. I asked questions and he . . . well, man, he just fended me off. All the same he struck me as a nice guy for all his side . . .'

'His side?' Gillian repeated, puzzled. Sometimes she could not understand Dirk at all. She had been trying to find a way to ask him why he had to *needle* poor Nanny. He seemed to enjoy shocking her and chuckled openly when she looked offended; almost as if he got pleasure from what he was doing. As if he enjoyed upsetting her, as if he was getting his revenge for something. And that was absurd for Dirk had only known her since he'd been coming down at week-ends and Nanny had never done anything to hurt him.

Now he was puzzling her still more. 'Peter has *side?* I don't get it, Dirk.'

Dirk laughed . . . flourishing his paint brush as if it was a weapon, ignoring the splashes of paint that landed on Gillian's face.

'Well, he reminded me of a doctor trying to tell me there's no hope.'

'No hope?'

Dirk grinned. 'Yah . . . no hope of recovery.'

'I don't understand.'

'Neither did I. I just had the feeling he was . . . well, it wasn't that he didn't *like* me for he was friendly enough. It was just something in the way he looked at me.'

'It could have been your hair . . .' Gillian teased.

'I'm proud of my hair.'

'Sure . . .' Gillian laughed. 'Man, I dig it . . .' she ducked in time as he swiped at her with his brush. 'Look, Dirk, we're not working, just talking. Let's get on.'

'You're the boss . . .' he said with a grin and turned away to paint enthusiastically.

As she painted, Gillian's thoughts whirled. She felt confused. Dirk she couldn't understand, neither could she understand Peter! That lovely girl and he had wanted to get rid of her. Dirk, saying Peter reminded him of a doctor trying to tell a frightening truth.

When they had finished and were tidying up, Gillian turned to Peter. 'Dirk's coming to dinner tonight, will you?'

95

Peter hesitated, saw the grin on Dirk's face, and accepted the invitation.

'Thanks, I have got a free evening.'

Gillian laughed. 'I knew that and I also know how you hate cooking. What were you going to have? Biscuits and cheese?'

Peter was cleaning his hands with turps and he looked at her. Was she in love with Dirk, he wondered, conscious of a feeling of uneasiness for her eyes were sparkling, her cheeks flushed, and she had that blossoming look so many women get when they are pregnant.

'Actually, Gillian, I have a chop in my fridge,' he said with dignity.

Dirk shouted with laughter. 'A chop in his fridge!'

Gillian smiled. 'Jolly good, Peter. You are progressing.'

'A very promising pupil,' he joked.

Bessie Beaky, the school mistress, came up, her face worried. She was in her late thirties, rather too plump, but with bright blue eyes, pretty blonde hair and a husky strangely-alluring voice.

'Sometimes it can be worrying if they're too promising.'

Peter turned to look at her and saw she was gazing at Mike Raines. He was tidying up, his young face earnest.

'He worries you?' Peter asked.

Bessie nodded. 'He's not brilliant, but he's flogging himself. He's determined to be top of the class. It's not that, though. It's this refusal to mix with the others. He walks alone.'

Peter smiled. 'Aren't you worrying too much? I mean, I always walked alone. I had few friends at school or afterwards. Anyhow it could be shock. The child probably misses his father.'

Bessie sighed. 'I'm sure it's not that. His father was always away, a salesman. Mike hardly knew him.' She gave a wry smile. 'I doubt if Bridget knew him much better. Her husband was a strange man, charming, bossy and selfish. Life had to revolve round him, no one else mattered. That's what hit poor Bridget so much when he was killed in a train smash, she had no idea about how to do anything. No, Peter, I don't think Mike misses his father. I wish I knew . . .'

'He's a nice little kid. We often have talks.'

Bessie put her hand on his arm. 'Maybe you could help us, Peter. Encourage him to talk and try to find out what is wrong.'

Peter smiled ruefully. 'Not so easy.'

'You'll try?' she looked up at him earnestly.

'I'll try,' he promised.

At Dirk's request, Peter drove him home. Dirk sat silently in the car, arms folded, head down on his chest. When Peter stopped, Dirk spoke abruptly.

'Aren't we mugs.'

'Mugs?'

Dirk nodded. 'The way we let Gill call the

tune. She cracks the whip in such a subtle way and we do just what she wants.'

Peter had to smile. 'I know but we needn't.'

Dirk opened his eyes and stared at the other man.

'Needn't we? Have you refused her anything?'

Peter hesitated and then told the truth. 'No.'

Dirk grinned. 'See what I mean? I don't know how she does it.'

'She'll make someone a good wife. A Vicar, perhaps.'

Dirk nodded, his appalling mass of hair swaying.

'I can see her ... running Sunday School, the Cubs, organizing bazaars, getting a great kick out of it all. Man, does she dig it. I just don't get it, somehow. What sort of life is it for a pretty girl?' He sounded exasperated. Had he suggested other ways for a pretty girl to live, Peter wondered, glancing at his companion.

'Come in and have a drink before we go down, Dirk,' he said as they got out of the car.

Dirk grinned. 'Sure. Thanks. How old did you say you were?'

Peter was startled. 'Thirty-five.'

'I get it. The awkward age. Me—I'm twenty. Also the awkward age. My heart bleeds for us both.'

'Why?' Peter was laughing but puzzled.

Dirk put his fingers together to form an

98

arch. 'Because we're neither fish nor fowl. I'm too young and you're too old. I reckon twenty-five is the best age.'

'I don't,' Peter told him. 'Mid-thirties is best for a man.'

'No, man, you're way out. Why, you're a square already. You're just not with it. You're not swinging.'

'I'm not sure that I want to swing,' Peter said and then thought how priggish it sounded. 'I have work I enjoy.'

'Ah!' Dirk waggled a finger. 'Here?'

'No, not here.'

Dirk chuckled. 'You are a close one. Okay, then, not here but you do have work you enjoy. Any idea how lucky you are? Fancy finding out in time what you want to do. See you ...' he finished hastily and hurried up the hill.

Peter went into his cottage, had a quick bath and changed into a sombre dark suit. He got drinks ready and waited for Dirk, wondering a little how he'd dress.

When Dirk walked in, it was even more bizarre than Peter, in his wildest moments, had dreamt of. Dirk wore skin-tight pink trousers and a tunic-like jacket of pale green, studded with yellow buttons. His mass of hair hung to his shoulders, his strangely beautiful face was half hidden.

Dirk grinned as Peter went to the tray of drinks.

'See what I mean? My crazy clothes and

yours! Why, anyone would think you were going to a funeral. We represent the two extremes. The young trying to impress, the oldie trying to hide.'

Peter had to laugh as he poured out the beer Dirk wanted.

'I've nothing to hide.'

'I didn't mean *that*. You want to hide *yourself*. I want to push myself forward so that I can be seen. You don't want to be seen. Why? Because you're scared. You're yellow, man, just plain yellow.'

'That's ridiculous,' Peter could not keep the note of irritation out of his voice. 'Gillian is always telling me I'm scared of being involved with people. It isn't that. It's simply that I prefer to remain single. My work . . .'

'Is your life?' Dirk grinned. 'What work? Or mustn't I ask?'

Peter smiled, his anger vanished. He found himself wondering if Dirk was really twenty years old. 'You may ask, Dirk,' Peter said, feeling absurdly like the lad's father and that would make him really old, 'but I won't answer.'

Dirk threw himself about as he laughed. 'Man, do I dig you . . .' he said as he finished the beer.

Peter stood up. 'Better get cracking. Nanny doesn't like her food to get cold.'

'Isn't that the funniest? Old Nanny, still working and loving it. Like something out of a

Jane Austen book. As square as the dodo and adoring Gill.'

'She doesn't hesitate to tear a strip off her if she deems it deserved,' Peter said as they walked out to the car.

'No, I know, and the odd thing is Gill does what she's told. It just doesn't make sense. She wouldn't do what I told her to do yet she does what Old Nanny says.'

'Maybe because she loves Nanny,' Peter said quietly.

'What difference does that make?'

'Well, Gillian knows that to Nanny she will always be the baby she brought up, she also knows Nanny loves her and wants to help her so she does what Nanny wants, just to make her happy. All the same, Gillian is an independent young person. She wouldn't do something she didn't want to do, just to please old Nanny.'

'Like marrying you?' Dirk asked with a grin.

'Marrying me?'

'M'm. Nanny approves.'

Peter laughed. 'Gillian warned me of that. Her parents approve, too.'

'And Gillian?'

They'd reached the Yeltons' house and were in the driveway. The door opened and Gillian stood there, so small and frail looking with her short dark hair, slanting eyes and welcoming smile.

'Hi . . .' Gillian shouted.

'Sorry we're late ...' Peter said, hastily getting out. 'Afraid we got talking over a beer.'

Gillian beamed. 'That's all right. We don't mind. Do come in. Gosh, Dirk,' she said and whistled softly. 'You're really something to look at.' She tucked her hand through his arm. 'Nanny really must see this. You look just as if you'd come from Top of the Pops.'

Laughing together, they went down the hall to the kitchen. Peter stood alone in the hall. Never before had he been so conscious of the age gap between himself and Gillian. Never before had it mattered so much.

CHAPTER NINE

Looking back later, Peter could never quite lay his finger on the exact date but he always thought it was just after this dinner party with the Yeltons, at which Dirk and Gillian acted like adolescents and he found himself siding with Anne and Philip Yelton and being classed definitely as an 'oldie', that things began to change.

No drastic change, of course, but something infinitely more subtle. As if Dirk's gay company had made Gillian see Peter as he really was.

But was he? he sometimes wondered. He didn't *feel* old, didn't *look* old, nor was he old!

No one in their senses could call thirty-five years 'old'.

The dinner had been pleasant enough. Dirk behaving quietly, listening politely to the other people's conversation but every now and then giving Gillian a special smile. Afterwards he and Gillian had gone to her sitting room and put on records and Peter, sitting quietly with the older Yeltons, could hear Dirk's laughter mingling with Gillian's.

'The young people of today,' Anne Yelton said, her voice wistful, 'are hard to understand. What she sees in that ... that ...' she smiled, and shrugged.

Her husband nodded. 'I often wonder if we shocked our parents as much as our children shock us. What d'you think of Thatcher, Peter?' He turned to Peter as to a man of his own age.

Peter hesitated. It was a pleasant early summer evening, with the garden looking attractive. The room was comfortably untidy and he felt relaxed.

'Actually I hardly know him,' he confessed. 'We had a drink and ... well, I have a feeling he's acting a part.'

'A con man?' Anne leaned forward excitedly, her face brightening.

Peter laughed. 'I don't think I'd say that or else he's an extremely good actor, no, I had a feeling he, well, he wanted to impress me. Not only me but the world.'

'I don't get it,' Philip Yelton said slowly, offering his wife and then Peter cigarettes. 'The way he behaves certainly doesn't impress *me*.'

They all laughed. 'Maybe I used the wrong word,' Peter said. 'Perhaps impress is unsuitable. He wants to be seen—to be noticed. It doesn't worry him what our opinion of him is so long as he is *seen*. Does that make sense?'

Philip Yelton loomed thoughtful. 'Be interesting to know his background. I think I know what you mean. One often meets it with the middle child. I don't think he's a bad lad, do you?'

Peter shook his head. 'No, most certainly not. I'd say he's a mixed-up kid. He says he's twenty but I doubt it.'

Anne Yelton looked worried. 'You don't think Gillian could be serious about him?' She looked at Peter. 'She is such a sweet child that I want her to make a happy marriage. She needs a more mature man to guide her ... she's so young.'

Peter smiled. 'Actually, Mrs. Yelton, I wouldn't have said that. I think Gillian is extremely mature. She is efficient as well as kind and has an amazing knack of making other people do things she wants them to do and yet leave them thinking they wanted to do it ...'

Philip Yelton was laughing, 'You are so
104

right, old man. That's Gillian exactly. No, Anne, I can't somehow see Gillian falling for Dirk. I guess she's sorry for him. She'd do anything to help someone she's sorry for . . .'

It was true. As the weeks passed, Peter remembered those words vividly. Slowly, subtly, Gillian left him to his own devices. She had launched him into his new life, seen he was progressing and decided it would be better for him to do what he had always said he liked: walk alone.

The odd thing was—he no longer wanted to walk alone! It wasn't that he didn't see as much of her as he had done before but somehow things were different. Her riding school had opened and he no longer went for his morning ride as Walkabout needed no exercise! He often met her on the beach and frequently took her dogs for a walk, as she had to leave them behind when she took out her pupils for a ride. They still met at dinner parties. At week-ends when Gillian was free she would join Dirk and Peter on the beach. They'd swim or just lie in the sun. She and Dirk never treated Peter as an *outsider* or suggested he was an *oldie* but Peter found himself sensitive on the subject and was constantly comparing himself with Dirk, and recognizing all the qualities in Dirk that Gillian obviously liked and that were notably missing in his own character. He felt there was a warm relationship between Dirk and Gillian, yet Dirk never said he loved her, or talked of the future.

Indeed Dirk talked little. He painted a lot, losing his temper and smashing his canvas or walking miles alone, his face sullen with disappointment. He wanted to be an artist and knew he wasn't one. He only, on the rare occasions when he spoke of himself, talked of the weekends. It was as if he only lived at week-ends, with his mop of hair and sad eyes, wearing off-beat clothes, delighting in shocking people.

Slowly, so slowly that Peter had not noticed it, his own whole reaction to those around him had changed. Where once he would have quickly dubbed Dirk a *phoney hippie* he now saw him as puzzled, unhappy and very young.

It was the same with other people. Often he visited old Mrs. Norris, sitting patiently, listening to her eager voice as she told him of the *good old days*, Peter knowing that Fiona had slipped out to meet her boy friend. Quietly, he encouraged Mrs. Norris to talk more and he learned she had five children but that Fiona was the only one who loved her. Mrs. Norris said once, her eyes filled with tears:

'I'm making a home for Fiona. She was the youngest and when her father died, I had to go out to work and she stayed with my sister. Fiona wasn't happy and she has felt insecure ever since. I know it makes her happy to know how much I need her. She's a good girl. If only she wasn't so clumsy ...' she added impatiently.

'This is a very quiet place,' he had said, glancing out of the window at the beach far below. Some children were racing in circles, there were small fishing boats bobbing about in the sea, but little else to look at, 'Wouldn't you be happier in a city?'

'I would but Fiona'd hate it. She loves the sea, she's always said so.'

'You've never thought of living with your other children?'

'Fiona needs me—she needs a home, and when I die, it'll be hers and a nice bit of money put away so she'll have no worries.'

But, Peter thought, still staring out of the window, what a price she'll have paid for it! Was Mrs. Norris telling the truth? Was she really doing this for Fiona? Was it a case of a double sacrifice?

One sunny afternoon, Peter felt restless. The garden was beginning to look like one. The tide was high, the water racing in to toss the waves in the air above the rocks, descending in myriads of tiny rainbow coloured drops. The cottage was quiet!

On an impulse, he drove down towards the village, past the school, and, driving past the bus station, saw a thin boy sitting patiently on a seat, hugging a large parcel.

It wasn't until he'd driven by that Peter

realized who it was: Mike Raines! Now what on earth, Peter wondered, could Mike be doing there? Normally he'd have been sitting on his own doorstep, waiting for his Mum.

Peter turned the car, not in the road but by going down side roads, so that he came towards Mike in the same direction as before. He slowed up and leaned out of the window to shout:

'Hey, Mike, want a lift?'

Peter saw the quick fear on the boy's face, the instinctive way he clutched the parcel, stood up and, for a moment, Peter thought the boy was going to run. But, instead, he came forward slowly, obviously with reluctance.

'I can get a bus, Mr. Richardson.'

'No trouble, Mike. I'm going to Penzance. Any help?' It was not the truth for Peter did not know *where* he was going, simply that he had to get out of the quiet cottage, but he'd suddenly made a wild guess that Mike was running away from home. But why? Mike adored his mother.

Mike's face lit up. 'Sure, Mr. Richardson, that's swell.'

He got in by Peter's side. They drove in silence as Peter searched for the right words to say.

'Know Penzance well? I've never been there before.'

Mike glanced at him. 'Neither have I.'

There was a long pause. 'Any particular

place you want me to drop you at?' Peter asked.

'Just anywhere will do,' Mike sighed. 'I've got to find some place to sleep.'

'I didn't know it was the holidays yet ...' Peter kept his voice casual as he swung round a corner. A lot of traffic about, he thought irritably, wondering what it would be like when the summer came.

Mike looked at him nervously. 'It isn't. I've left school.'

'Oh,' Peter said and left the matter there for a few minutes, then went on: 'What does your Mum think? You're not very old, you know.'

'She doesn't know yet.' Mike stared straight ahead. 'I'm going to phone her from Penzance.'

'I see. She'll miss you, Mike ...' Peter turned to look at the small boy and watched his eyes well with tears.

'I've got to get a job, Mr. Richardson,' Mike's voice was uneven. 'I've got to. Mum finds it hard to pay the rent and ... and I am the man of the family.' The boy's voice trembled and he said nothing more.

'I see.' Peter didn't lift his foot from the accelerator and was careful to keep his voice even. 'There are a few obstacles, Mike, old chap, I'm afraid.'

'Oh ... obstacles?'

'M'm. You see there is a law that insists that children have to stay at school until a certain age. You're nowhere near that age yet. Another obstacle is that no one's allowed to give anyone of your age a full time job. Only a part time one.'

Peter saw that Mike had twisted in the seat, tucking his legs under him so that he could turn and look at Peter.

'What's a part time job?'

'Well, you only work so many hours a day. After or before school, it can be.'

'Would I get paid much?' Peter heard with relief the prepared acceptance in Mike's voice.

'Not much but it adds up. Why d'you want to earn money?'

'But I must, Mr. Richardson,' Mike's voice was earnest. 'That's what they all said when Dad ... when Dad ... well, when Dad's and Mum's relations came to see us. They said I must grow up fast and take Dad's place and look after Mum. They said I was the man of the family and must never forget it. I didn't know what they meant so I asked lots of people and everyone said the man of the family must have a good job and pay for everything ...'

'But hardly at your age ...'

'Does that make a difference?' Mike sounded surprised.

'A great difference. That's what your relatives meant—that when you grew up and became a man, you must always think of your mother.'

110

'You mean, I don't have to look after her *now*? How old d'you have to be to become a man, Mr. Richardson?'

'Well, it depends.' Peter drew up beside a café. 'I'm starving. Feel like some chips or ice cream?'

'Sure.'

Mike followed the tall thin man into the shop. They had a table in the window, looking down on Penzance, the crowded streets far below them, the harbour full of ships and yachts.

'You asked me what age you must be to become a man, Mike. Some boys earn their living and become a "man" at sixteen. Others who are ambitious and want really good jobs, stay on at school until they're eighteen or nineteen.'

'I want a really good job and then Mum can stop working.'

'Good. Like being a doctor or an architect or . . .'

'I'm going to be a scientist. Miss Beaky says I haven't many brains but I work hard.'

Peter laughed. 'Your Mum'll be proud of you. Look, Mike, how about this for an idea? Get a part time job for after school hours and save the money in the post office. Then if ever Mum is in trouble and can't pay a bill, you could pay it for her . . .'

Mike's eyes shone. 'Why that's great, Mr. Richardson.'

His face changed, became miserable. 'But where can I get a part time job.'

'Easily. I'll give you one. I need help in my garden, my shoes need cleaning, you can wash the lunch dishes . . .' Peter thought fast, trying to find logical-sounding suggestions. 'I'll pay you and we'll put it straight in the post office once a week and you'll know it's there.'

'Gee . . . when can I start work?'

Peter called for the bill, glanced at his watch, 'Well, if we don't meet too much traffic we'll get home before your Mum does so she won't be worried and you can start work tomorrow. Okay?'

'Okay . . .' Mike was on his feet at once, his unhappy face bright, his hair rumpled as he beamed. As they got into the car, he said: 'I didn't want to get a job, you know.'

Peter gave him a quick smile. 'I know. I think it was brave of you, Mike.'

'I only wanted to help Mum . . .'

Peter rumpled the boy's hair. 'Your Mum will be proud of you, Mike, but next time you have a problem like that, promise to come and ask me.'

'Oh, I will, Mr. Richardson . . .' Mike bounced happily on the seat of the car, hugging his parcel. 'I most certainly will.'

As they reached Pendennis and then the hillside, Peter saw Bridget at her gate, looking worriedly up the hill. Gillian was with her.

'Look, Mike,' Peter said quickly. 'You can

112

tell your Mum later about what happened. Skip up to the house with your bundle— clothes, is it? I thought so and I'll keep them from asking questions.'

Mike grinned. 'Okedoke.'

Peter stopped the car by the side of the white gate and got up quickly, 'Hi ... sorry we're late, Bridget. Hope you weren't worried ...'

He saw she had been crying as he moved closer giving Mike a chance to slip round the back and to the cottage.

'All my fault. I should have rung and told you we were going to Penzance. Gillian ...' He turned to her where she stood still, her eyes puzzled. 'I was wondering ... look, I've had a lot of hospitality from you so I wondered if you'd have dinner with me tonight in Cudjack. I see there's a new Chinese place.'

From the corner of his eye Peter saw that Mike had returned, was standing by his mother's side, sliding his hand into hers and she was smiling down at him, her eyes filled with tears.

'Gillian,' Peter added hastily, 'I need your advice about some of the plants. Would you come up with me, now?'

'Of course.' She sounded as puzzled as she looked and got in the car by his side. As he carefully turned it he saw that Mike and his mother were walking slowly up to their cottage, hand in hand.

Gillian turned to stare at him. 'And what exactly does it all mean?'

Peter grinned and told her the whole story: 'Poor kid,' he finished, 'he felt he was letting his Mum down because he wasn't being the Man of the Family. That's why he's been so strange. If he's the Man of the Family, I suppose he felt he should act differently, work hard, not play about with the other kids.'

'So you've given him a job . . .' Gillian said slowly, 'Won't he be a nuisance?'

'Mike—a nuisance?' Peter laughed. 'At least, I'll have someone to talk to . . .'

'Peter . . . are you lonely?'

He shrugged. 'Sometimes, aren't we all?'

She put her hand on his arm. 'Why do you stay here if you're so unhappy? Why don't you go back and face up to things?'

Before he could answer, a small dog shot across the road. Peter jammed on the brakes and swerved, just avoiding the dog who scuttled out of sight.

As he straightened the car, Peter swore silently and said aloud: 'Of all the crazy . . . why don't people train their dogs!'

'I know,' Gillian agreed. 'That was close. Do you really want my advice about the plants, Peter?'

'No,' he laughed, 'I wanted to give Mike a chance to tell his mother the truth.'

'Okay. Then drop me here as I must hurry home. What time shall I expect you tonight?'

'Seven all right?'

She smiled and got out of the car as he stopped. She turned away and then looked back at him.

'D'you know something, Peter? You're learning fast.'

Before he could ask her what she meant, she had waved her hand and was running down the side of the hill towards her home.

CHAPTER TEN

As Gillian dressed for dinner she realized Peter's invitation was the first time he had treated her as a woman—as an adult. Always before there had been a friendly but rather condescending air as if she was a child and he, the schoolmaster!

She held up her dresses before her and stared into the mirror, mentally comparing herself with Peter's girl friend.

No one could compete with Lucille, Gillian told herself, so why waste time trying? The thing was to wear something that suited her!

But what did suit her? She was so thin and her skin was brown from the sea air. Her dark hair, cut short so that it would not be a nuisance, was difficult to make look attractive! Finally she decided on a magnolia red sheath frock, very simple but eye-catching.

Her mother came into the room, trying to hide her obvious delight. 'How sweet of Peter to ask you out like this ...'

Her mother drooled on and on until Gillian wanted to scream. She knew her mother couldn't help it but if only she would stop trying to matchmake! One day, Gillian knew, she would meet the right man, marry him and be happy ever after—if only her mother would leave her alone!

Peter arrived on the dot. Accepted a drink from Gillian's mother and then firmly but diplomatically edged them both towards the door. Gillian's mother followed them outside, her face one huge smile, as she said she hoped they'd have a lovely evening.

As the car drew away, Gillian gave an enormous sigh and Peter glanced down at her with a smile.

'Don't worry, Gillian, lots of mothers do that.'

'But it's so embarrassing. Anyone would think you were about to propose to me ...' Gillian tried to laugh.

For once, Peter didn't smile. 'What would you say if I did?' he asked quietly.

Gillian was startled. She sat upright, turning her surprised face towards him. 'You're joking ...'

He laughed then. 'Of course I'm joking. Don't look so terrified. I just wondered how you'd feel about marrying an oldie.'

'You're not an oldie.'

'Dirk thinks so and I thought you did.'

'Oh, Dirk!' There was a note of exasperation in Gillian's voice. 'I just can't understand him sometimes.'

'That makes two of us.'

'Peter—what d'you really think of Dirk? I know my parents think he's the end but . . .'

'No, I think they quite like him but he puzzles them—just as he does us . . .' Peter said thoughtfully, slowing up at the traffic lights before the old stone bridge. 'It seems to me sometimes that there are two Dirks. The one I like and the exhibitionist that drives me mad.'

'You're so right Peter. That's how I feel. When Dirk relaxes, he's a totally different person and then—just like switching on a light, he changes and starts showing off, trying to shock people. Why?'

The car moved forward slowly, gathering speed as they climbed the slope on which the village was built and reached the open moors, now covered with golden gorse.

If we knew why, it might solve a lot of problems.' Peter hesitated. 'I think your parents are a bit worried in case you're serious about Dirk.'

Gillian was startled. 'Me? Serious? you mean with Dirk. We've never even thought of it. I mean, he isn't . . . well, he just doesn't . . .'

Peter saw that Gillian was blushing. He

117

wondered why.

'I don't think he's the marrying kind,' Gillian went on. 'Yet he needs a wife.'

'Needs?'

'M'm. He's terribly unsure of himself. He needs an adoring wife to bolster up his ego but then most men do.'

Peter, deftly unravelling the car from a traffic block as they approached Cudjack, smiled, 'Do I?'

'Of course. It stands out a mile,' Gillian said laughing. 'No, seriously, Peter, I can't imagine marrying anyone like Dirk unless I felt he really needed me.'

'That's no reason for marriage, Gillian. It could only be a failure and Dirk would end up more insecure than ever.'

'I wonder . . .' Gillian gazed ahead dreamily as Peter drove through the crowded small town, looking for a parking place. 'I really wonder.'

'Then don't,' Peter snapped irritably, parking the car in a narrow cobbled alley, 'for it would never work.'

They went into the small restaurant in silence, going down the stairs to the warm crowded room, being met by a polite head waiter, led to a small table, partly obscured from the other tables by a discreetly placed screen.

Peter asked Gillian what she would like and then ordered drinks, offered her a cigarette

118

and gave a wry smile.

'Sorry I bit your head off outside, Gillian, but I've seen marriages based on sacrifice, one party wanting to help the other and ending up with everyone, often more than the original two, being unhappy. You have to have a better reason than that for marriage.'

'What sort of reason?' She rested her elbows on the table, her chin in her cupped hands as she looked up at him.

'Well . . . well . . .' Peter looked round at the tables filled with groups of laughing people, or occasionally a couple, eating but not talking.

Gillian chuckled. 'That's not a very helpful answer. What reason would make you marry, Peter?'

He frowned. 'You know my views on marriage. With my work . . .'

'But if your work was different? I mean, if it didn't mean so much to you? Then what would make you marry?'

Peter tried to think. 'Honestly I don't know.' He tugged at the lobe of his ear. 'I suppose if I found I couldn't bear to live without her. I can't imagine it . . .' He gave an odd laugh. 'You learn to live without love.'

'Didn't anyone love you when you were a child?'

Gillian's gentle voice caused Peter to be more frank than he would normally have been.

'Only my grandmother and she died when I was twelve. My parents were always abroad as

I told you. I rarely saw them. I meant nothing to them—and they meant nothing to me.'

'They did, didn't they, Peter? Poor you. No wonder you're scared of getting involved.'

His face felt uncomfortably hot. 'I am not scared. I just want to . . .'

'I know. Walk alone. D'you honestly think that's the solution?'

Peter hesitated. 'It's mine,' he said firmly as the waiter arrived with the huge menus. 'Now, what d'you fancy, Gillian?'

It was a pleasant meal. They drank wine and stopped discussing serious matters, instead they joked and laughed. Gillian found herself wishing the evening need never end for this was Peter at his nicest. Often on the beach he would suddenly go silent; even turn away and ignore her and Dirk, if he was there, as if they moved in different worlds but here he was relaxed, at ease, as if this was the life he was accustomed to . . .

When they were leaving the restaurant, Gillian hesitated but there was no means of avoiding the two women, sitting at a small table near the door.

'Watch out, Peter . . .' Gillian said, turning to the tall thin man by her side. 'We'll be passing the village gossips. They've been away on holiday so you haven't met them yet.'

He chuckled. 'Thanks for the warning. Are they really so bad?'

'You've no idea! I'll have to introduce

you . . .'

'All right . . .'

As they walked towards them, the two elderly women were watching them, obviously having seen them earlier, and even more obviously bubbling over with curiosity.

'Why Gillian dear, how nice you look. Quite a change from the way you usually dress . . .' the oldest, fattest, most malicious-looking one said.

'Thanks, Miss Owen,' Gillian managed a smile. 'I hope you had a good holiday.'

Gladys Owen frowned, 'Not really. Weather appalling, hotel service poor and Natalie here was fool enough to be ill. It spoilt everything.'

Her companion, as thin and sweet-looking as her friend was the reverse, smiled, 'Oh, it wasn't as bad as that, Gladys. A most delightful little hotel, such charming people, and I wasn't ill long.' Her sweetness had an unnatural saccharine-quality, Peter thought, as the women stared curiously at him. Both were obviously comfortably off, wearing expensive silk suits, matching hats, both had white hair touched a smokey blue, both were over-made-up, both typical of small communities where there were always to be found people who delighted in causing trouble.

'And who's your charming friend, Gillian?' Miss Owen asked, her voice impatient as if she considered she had been kept waiting too long for the answer.

121

'This is Mr. Richardson,' Gillian said. 'He's here for a few months and has got Mrs. Trent's cottage.'

'That terrible place?' Gladys Owen sniffed. 'So small—not suitable for a gentleman . . .'

'You're from London?' Natalie Jones chimed in eagerly. 'How bored you must be here. You do play bridge, of course?'

Gillian gently nudged Peter but he was already prepared.

'Not often.'

'Pete . . . Mr. Richardson is an author,' Gillian said quickly. 'He often works at night.'

'I see . . .' Gladys Owen looked at Peter carefully and then at Gillian. 'But you must come to dinner, some time, Mr. Richardson. Of course, we'll ask Gillian, too,' she added with a coy smile.

'I'll be delighted . . .' Peter said and then they managed to escape.

In the car they stared at one another and both laughed.

'You can imagine what will happen now . . .' Gillian said. 'Miss Owen is the greatest gossip in the neighbourhood and what Miss Jones doesn't know she invents. Tomorrow everyone will be talking about us, I'm afraid.'

Peter started the car, slowly reversing. 'Does it really matter?'

'It depends if you mind. I don't.'

'Neither do I. What a perfect night.'

Gillian twisted round to look at him. 'In a

hurry to get home?'

'No. Why?'

'Well, about twenty miles along the coast there is the most gorgeous lookout. We can see right over on both sides and with this moon!'

Peter smiled. 'Fine. You direct me.'

As he drove, he remembered how Dirk had said that they were always doing what Gillian wanted.

Even now he was doing what she suggested. In some ways, she was rather bossy. He hadn't realized it at the beginning but he had felt very differently then. He could remember vividly the shock he had felt when David Rugg had told him he had to take six months holiday and be buried alive in the depths of the Cornish coast. He had been stunned, temporarily, then horrified at the empty quietness of the cottage, the unending boring aimless days so that Gillian's manoeuvres had been not only acceptable but very welcome. Gillian had shown him how to live under such difficult circumstances.

'I'm glad you sorted out Mike's problem,' Gillian said abruptly.

'It sorted itself.'

'You're being modest.' Gillian smiled at him. 'Think he'll be all right now?'

Peter hesitated. I'm not sure. I did think I'd try to have a chat with his mother. I don't think Mike's part time job will solve all his problems. I want to ask her to give Mike more responsibility, to make him feel he is helping her.'

'In other words, taking the place of his Dad?'

'Yes. He has this complex about being the Man of the House and he won't be completely happy unless he feels he is doing his duty. There are lots of little things she can ask him to do, and pretend she can't do them herself. It could make a big differencc.'

'Peter ...' Gillian began and stopped. Even with him in this relaxed mood, she lacked the courage to ask him outright how he knew so much about people. How many men would worry about a child like Mike and his problems? 'Peter, Mike's Mum is very pretty so watch out. The gossips are back ...'

Peter laughed. 'So they are. Oh well, if it makes them happy gossiping, I don't mind.'

They parked, under Gillian's instructions, on the flat top of the cliff. It was indeed beautiful. The great expanse of sea with the waves rolling in, white and furious, the wide splash of moonshine turning the water into molten silver, the stillness only disturbed by the sound of the sea, the lovely line of the coast.

'We seem so far from London ...' Peter began.

'You miss it?'

'No, strangely enough, I don't.'

'I'm glad ...' Gillian smiled at him. 'You're

looking much happier than you did when you first came here.'

He smiled back. 'I am much happier thanks to you, Gillian. Thanks entirely to you . . .'

She was completely unprepared for what happened next because he moved fast, his hands on her shoulders as he stooped down and kissed her.

'You're very sweet, Gillian . . .' he said softly and then spoiled everything by adding: 'A very sweet child.'

CHAPTER ELEVEN

Walking along the sands with the dogs racing ahead Gillian found it impossible to forget Peter's kiss. She tried to rationalize her thoughts. After all, what was a kiss? She was twenty years old and it was certainly not the first time she had been kissed! Even Dirk, with surprisingly shy clumsiness, had kissed her. Yet the way Peter had kissed her, had been different.

Or would it have been different, she told herself as she stared moodily out at the waves racing in, if he hadn't spoiled everything by those last words:

'A sweet child.'

Now why had he said that? Had he suddenly been scared, afraid that she, a naïve country girl, might read more into that innocent little kiss than he had meant? Or had he said it truthfully because that was how he saw her: 'a sweet child'?

Whatever reason, it had spoiled everything. You didn't marry or jump into bed with a man simply because he kissed you—but then, neither did a girl of twenty see it as a compliment to be called a 'sweet child'.

Naturally she told no one, least of all hcr mother, whose eyes would have shone excitedly and who would have started immediately to plan the wedding! All the same, Gillian could not forget the kiss and it made her try to avoid meeting Peter when she could.

That of course, was easier said than done, for Peter as the only bachelor in the immediate neighbourhood, was asked out to dinner every night and invariably Gillian was asked as well. Sometimes she wondered if he had changed, too, for a wall seemed to have suddenly grown up between them. They were friendly but no longer relaxed when alone together. It was almost as if both were on guard. A strange new feeling for Gillian and as the days passed and became busier with the holiday makers coming for rides as well as the regular riding lessons to be given she gradually pushed the kiss out of her mind.

Or thought he had. But it returned vividly one afternoon when, running down to the

126

beach alone for a quick swim between riding lessons, Gillian skidded to a halt as the hot sand touched her bare feet. She turned instantly and hurried home but she could not forget the two figures standing down by the water's edge talking.

Peter—his head bent slightly towards his companion, the beautiful Lucille! Neither were in swim suits. Peter was wearing an open-necked white shirt and white flannels, which meant that the Pursers had asked him round to play tennis, as Gillian had suggested to them the week before. Lucille was in an elborate play-suit of emerald green that intensified her long slender legs, and her composed, slightly arrogant air. She was looking at Peter, her hand on his arm possessively.

Did Peter kiss Lucille, Gillian found herself wondering. Of course he did, she told herself angrily. He's known her for so long and there was one thing for sure—after he kissed Lucille. Peter would most certainly not call her 'a sweet child'!

Gillian changed quickly, surprised at how upset she felt for Peter was just a friend. If he loved Lucille that was his business. In any case, why was Lucille here? Somehow it wasn't the sort of seaside resort Gillian would have imagined Lucille would like! Surely somewhere more exotic with palm trees and humid air. Not this quiet wind-blown

127

backwater as Lucille obviously saw it. Had she come down at Peter's invitation?'

Peter had been just as surprised as Gillian when he met Lucille. He had been on his way to tennis with the Pursers and, aware of curious eyes and eager ears, he had suggested they stroll down over the sand.

'What on earth are you doing here?' he demanded.

She smiled. 'I came to scc you, of course. Why else?'

His temper had begun to flare up, 'This is ridiculous, Lucille.'

'Is it? Ridiculous? To want to be near the man you love? Peter, grow up. I love you and I've got to make you see sense. You were a fool to come here. Oh yes, I *know* about the blackouts, I *knew* you needed a holiday but six months buried in the drab depths of Cornwall is absurd. Rugg is behind this, he's ambitious and you're too bright for his liking. He wanted you out of the way.' Her voice changed and became angry: 'Then there is me. He doesn't approve of me, does he?'

Peter turned away, so angry he could hardly speak.

'Who does?'

Her hand gripped his arm tight. 'You do— only you won't admit it. That's why I'm here. To talk some sense into you.'

'Lucille ... will you please remove your hand from my arm,' Peter his voice slightly unsteady as he fought the anger that rushed through him. 'We are in full view of the village gossips' cottage and no doubt they are watching us through binoculars.'

'Undoubtedly,' Lucille chuckled but she let go of his arm. 'I've given them plenty to gossip about.'

He swung round. 'What the . . . ?'

She smiled. 'Oh, just subtle hints.'

'No one here knows what . . .'

'You are? I discovered that as a result of skilful questioning.' She laughed. 'But why? What have you to hide?'

'Nothing at all. It was Roger's . . .'

'Roger again. All right, I'll respect your desire for anonymity. There's already quite a lot of gossip about you, Peter dear. Or perhaps you don't know?'

He turned away and began to walk up towards the street. Lucille followed him, her long beautiful legs easily covering the ground at his speed. 'I am staying at the Lamb and Cross and I hear things,' she went on, her voice amused. 'What about a certain widow who has a son who calls you Dad?'

'He does not . . .'

'Maybe not to you, Peter, but all the locals know that he hopes you'll marry his mother. Then there's a girl called Jacquie. You go there at least once a week . . .'

'I take her young brother, Ginger, to judo classes and when I drive him back, she asks me in for a meal. She knows I have to cook for myself and . . .'

'But you don't have to . . .' Lucille's voice seemed to crack a little. 'You don't have to stay here. Look, Peter, it is your life . . .'

He stopped dead as he reached the road and turned to her. She had never seen him look so angry before.

'Yes, it is my life, Lucille, and as I have told you a hundred times before, nothing to do with you. I am not in love with you nor will I ever marry you. Is that clear?'

Unthinkingly he caught her by both her arms and shook her. 'I asked you—is that clear? I want to be left alone . . .'

Lucille was a perfect actress though somewhat corny, Peter thought with disgust, as he watched her eyes fill with tears, saw the way her mouth trembled as she said:

'But I love you, Peter.'

'Oh for crying out loud!' he said. 'Come off it, Lucille, it's not *me* you love.' He let go of her and stalked off down the road. He wanted to go back to his cottage but the Pursers were expecting him. He'd not played tennis for many years and they were pleasant people.

He walked past the big mansion that was now a school. The grounds were full of children, playing different games. The sun shone down and there was a feeling of peacefulness about the place. It seemed far removed from the rat race of the cities.

Or it had been peaceful, he thought angrily, as he walked along. How Lucille had the cheek . . . but then she had an arrogance that surpassed anything he had ever met. She wanted him as a husband. Not because she loved him but for two other reasons: one, the fact that she had to chase and overcome him. There was something predatory about her, she reminded him of a slinky cheetah. The second reason was that he was a rich man, that he had what she called a 'fortune' inherited from his parents. Money invested and often forgotten, though sometimes Peter had the uneasy feeling that it should be used for some specific purpose. He smiled wryly, he'd better not let Gillian know about the money or she would persuade him to give it to her favourite charity!

He reached the Pursers' house, a pleasant white building with a lovely garden and well-cared-for tennis courts. As he went into the driveway, he wondered how long Lucille had booked in at the Lamb and Cross and what her next move would be. She was not one to be easily discouraged. Perhaps he should go away for a few days and then maybe she would read between the lines and take the hint. Maybe! But most unlikely, he told himself as he joined the group of people waiting for him.

'Hope I'm not late but I met someone . . .' he began.

Mrs. Purser, a too-thin woman with

unbounding energy, smiled, 'I know. She is very lovely, Peter. I gather you are old friends.'

Peter was startled. 'You've met her? When . . . how long has she been here? I had no idea . . .'

Mrs. Purser chuckled. 'I know. She told me she wanted to surprise you. She came yesterday and hadn't booked in anywhere. I happened to be in the post office when she asked which was the best placc to go to and I suggested the Lamb and Cross. They are very crowded but I've known Joe Gould for many years and he managed it.'

'Oh, Mum, Mr. Richardson's come to play tennis not talk,' sixteen year old Wendy Purser said with a frown. She was an ardent, but not good, player and Peter had half-promised to coach her because, as she said, her parents got impatient with her.

'Like learning to drive a car.' Wendy had said with a quick smile. 'Never let your father teach you.'

Meanwhile Lucille had dabbed her eyes and looked sad as she walked by the gossips' cottage which was a pretty place but rather too big to be called a 'cottage'. Mrs. Purser, whom she had met the day before had pointed it out to her.

'Watch your step if you meet them,' she had said. 'They're gossips and they cause quite a bit of trouble.'

Inwardly Lucille smiled and as she passed

the big bow windows, she mopped her eyes again. She was sure the two women who lived there would have been watching the scene on the beach. That would have given them something to talk about, Lucille thought happily. The dramatic little scene, her hand on Peter's arm, the obvious quarrel as he walked away and she followed him. Then when he grabbed her arms and shook her and then went off, leaving her to dry her tears . . .

Oh yes, Lucille found herself chuckling, the gossips would most certainly have something to talk about!

A few discreet questions had told her quite a lot about Peter. It was obvious that the biggest menace was that extraordinary looking girl, Gillian Yelton. She had a strange beauty and there was obviously more between her and Peter than he would admit. Why else had the girl turned tail and fled when she saw them talking on the beach?

Lucille made her way to the Yelton's house. It was easy enough to recognize because of the stables at the back. She found Gillian and Brummel getting the horses ready for the next lessons.

Gillian was wearing jodhpurs and a white shirt. She looked startled and, Lucille thought, dismayed when she saw her visitor.

'I'm so sorry I can't ask you in . . .' Gillian was saying, 'I've got pupils due in ten minutes and . . .'

Lucille smiled. 'That's all right. I quite understand. What I have to say won't take long. Is there anywhere quiet?'

Gillian hesitated and then turned to the groom. 'I'll be in the summerhouse if they come early, Brummel.'

He nodded, his eyes bright with curiosity as he gazed at Lucille. His face was old and weather-beaten but she saw the admiration in his eyes. He wasn't too old to appreciate beauty, she thought complacently.

Gillian, feeling absurdly nervous, led the way across the beautifully-kept lawn to a small sheltered summer house. She unfolded two canvas chairs and indicated one.

'Please sit down, Miss . . . Miss . . .'

Lucille smiled. 'Please call me Lucille. I hate formalities and after all, we are both friends of Peter, aren't we?'

Gillian stared at her and was afraid. Then the next moment ashamed of the fear. What harm could this beautiful girl do her? Why should she want to hurt her?

'Yes,' Gillian said flatly.

'You're very young . . .'

'I am not,' Gillian replied immediately. 'I'm twenty . . .'

'I find it hard to believe. You look a mere child.'

Gillian closed her eyes. How she hated that word. Was that what Peter called her if he mentioned her to Lucille? That was how he

134

saw her.

'Well, it's the truth,' Gillian said sullenly. 'I know I don't look it but . . .'

'My dear . . .' Lucille's voice was gentle. Too gentle for Gillian's liking so she braced herself for the attack. 'You are such a sweet child, so naïve, so young that I am really angry about the whole thing.'

Gillian opened her eyes quickly. 'Angry? The whole thing?'

'Yes, Gillian. The gossip going around. It's so cruel. But then people can be very cruel. I sympathize with you. You are young, live in this backwater, probably meet few men. Peter is extremely attractive, sophisticated and kind. I know you are not running after him but . . .'

Two bright flags of colour flamed in Gillian's cheeks.

'They're saying I'm chasing him?'

'I'm afraid so, my dear,' Lucille's voice was again gentle. 'So wrong and so cruel.'

'You know I'm not chasing him?'

Lucille smiled. 'Of course I do. You're not that type of girl, Gillian. The point is that Peter is very embarrassed about it all.' She put up her hand as Gillian began to speak: 'I know, I know. He always says he despises gossip and doesn't care what people say about him but that's not true. He's very sensitive, indeed. He's in a most awkward position as you can see. He's fond of you, Gillian, that's obvious to everyone and he's far too kind to tell you the truth.'

'The truth?' Gillian found it surprisingly difficult to speak. She was bewildered. Lucille was being so friendly and helpful. And Peter was embarrassed? Lucille should know Peter best, she'd known him for so long.

'Yes, that everyone says you are chasing him and that you are even talking of marrying him . . .'

'They're not . . .' Gillian jumped up. 'Why, there's no . . .' She stopped and her hand went to her mouth in dismay. It was quite possible, and more than probable, that her mother had been talking! Oh, very diplomatically, of course, but nevertheless it was possible that she had hinted at the romance, making her wishful thinking become a fact.

Lucille nodded. 'Sit down, my dear. I won't be long. I know it's not your fault and I hate having to tell you this but . . . well, Peter and I . . .'

Gillian drew a deep breath. 'He told me his work came first. That he would never marry . . .'

'Poor Peter. His usual excuse. Unfortunately, at the moment there are obstacles to our marriage, Gillian. That is why he's been so ill . . .' Lucille stopped dead. 'Oh, dear, I shouldn't have told you that . . .'

'He came here because he'd been ill?'

'Yes. So frustrated, poor darling, and he loves me so much. He's here to rest and I can

136

assure you that the worst thing that can happen to him is to be involved in scandal or gossip. He's supposed to lead a quiet life here . . . That's why I was so glad when he wrote and told me how kind you'd been to him and helpful. I'm sorry it's turned out this way.' She stood up and Gillian followed suit.

'One last thing, Gillian,' Lucille said softly. 'You're a nice girl and I don't want you hurt. At your age, it is very easy to have a crush on an older man. Peter is attractive and I wouldn't blame you in the least.'

'Peter is just a friend.' Gillian said quickly. 'I've never thought of him in any other way.'

Lucille smiled. 'I'm so glad, Gillian. I would hate you to be hurt. That's all, then . . .'

They walked together over the grass towards the stables. Gillian saw that her three pupils were waiting for her.

'What can I do?' she asked impulsively, turning to the girl by her side.

Lucille smiled again. 'Try to avoid being seen alone with Peter. It would help him a lot if you had a boy friend. There must be someone.'

'You mean then the gossips would stop linking my name with Peter's?'

'Exactly. How clever of you, Gillian. I'm sure you would do anything you could to help my poor Peter. He needs help and there is little I can do . . . Now I'll say goodbye.'

'Are you staying long?'

137

'Unfortunately no. Peter has begged me to but I have other commitments. I was worried by what he said in his letters so I came down to straighten things out for him.'

'And you have?'

Lucille smiled at her. 'Yes, I have. I feel very relieved, Gillian. I knew you would understand and that I could rely on you to help us both.'

CHAPTER TWELVE

After the afternoon of tennis, Peter on his way home stopped at the public telephone box outside the post office. The two elderly sisters had asked him for dinner that night.

'I'm sorry about tonight but would you forgive me . . .' he began, wondering what sort of excuse he could make. He had never been good at telling white lies.

The quiet, docile sister laughed. A sympathetic but coy sound. 'Oh, Mr. Richardson, we *quite* understand. As soon as we met her, I said to my sister, "I don't expect Mr. Richardson will come to dinner tonight." And I don't blame you either, you know. She is very beautiful.'

Peter caught his breath. Lucille had certainly got around.

'It's very good of you, Miss Thomas, some other time I hope.'

'Of course, Mr. Richardson, of course . . .'

Peter put down the receiver and stood still for a moment. He could feel the anger seeping through him slowly. He clenched and unclenched his hands. He had wanted to postpone the dinner in case Lucille came in search of him. She was quite capable of behaving in a way to embarrass him. She had already succeeded! Well, when she came to the cottage that night, he was going to have it out with her. This ridiculous chase must end. He was tired to death of it and somehow he must find a way to convince her that she was flogging a dead horse. Perhaps he could pretend there was another woman?

He wondered if she would believe him. In any case, who was there? No, he wasn't a good liar and Lucille would soon see through the story. He must just make her realize that he had no intention at all of getting married. Ever. Most particularly not to her!

He had a tin of salmon so he opened it for his meal. It was a hot humid night and he sat on his chair just outside the front door, waiting.

But she didn't come.

It was very quiet on the hillside. Dirk only came at week-ends. The cottages lower down were still also. Yet he had only to walk to the top of the hill and glance down the other side to see the holiday-makers hurrying to and from their places of entertainment like a pack of ants, many were still on the beach. One thing they rarely, if ever, found their way down his side of the hill.

How still it was, he thought. He smoked his pipe and watched the few fishing vessels out at sea. The water came racing in with powerful certainty of where it was going, only to reach the rocks where the water splashed and threw water drops high in the air.

The powerful certainty of where it was going ... he repeated the words. What had made him say that, he wondered.

How many people knew where they were going? Lucille obviously thought she did. But did *he*? Where was he going?

He got up, impatient with himself. What a stupid question to ask. He was perfectly happy, he liked his work, he had enough money so that he had no financial problems. What more could he want?

He waited until ten o'clock, still wondering if Lucille would turn up after dark, deliberately ensuring that everyone knew! He wondered where she was. Had one of her 'new friends' invited her to dinner? But if so, wouldn't they have asked him, too?

It was a long time before he slept. First he heard the roar of Dirk's scooter and realized that next day would be Saturday. He would go down to see Lucille and make her understand—this sort of waiting was too exhausting.

140

In the morning, he walked to the Lamb and Cross. Mrs. Ford, who worked there part-time, looked at him with condemning eyes:

'She's gone, Mr. Richardson. Very upset she was, too,' she added. 'Poor girl. Weeping and all.'

'Weeping?' Peter stared at her, unbelieving. It was fairly dark in the low-ceilinged hall but it was plain that Mrs. Ford blamed him for Lucille's tears. 'But why?'

Mrs. Ford sniffed noisily. She had a florid round face and rather a big nose, a mouth that drooped at the corners and a habit of talking about her ailments.

'*You* should know that if anyone does, Mr. Richardson. Shaking the poor girl like that in front of people . . . proper scared she was, too, when she came back later and began to pack.'

'Shaking her . . .' Peter began and then remembered. He began to laugh. 'Why, that was nothing. Lucille always was a good actress.'

Mrs. Ford sniffed even louder. 'That's as maybe but I know tears when I see 'em and she was really broken-hearted. I'm surprised at you, Mr. Richardson, I really am. I thought you were a kind man but how you could hurt such a beautiful girl beats me.'

'Look,' Peter took a deep breath. 'I've known Lucille for twelve years, Mrs. Ford, and I assure you that I could not hurt her, even if I tried. She's annoyed with me because I won't do what she wants. That's all.'

He turned and walked out, very conscious of the aura of disapproval he'd left behind him. Now what was Lucille up to, he wondered. Making him look a monster who shook a girl in front of people and broke her heart! At least she had gone. There was that much to be thankful for!

Walking back—it was odd, he thought, how playing golf had made him accustomcd to walking. He no longer used his car for travelling short distances.

The big setter came racing to greet him, followed by the other two dogs and then Gillian.

'Hi . . .' he greeted her. 'I'm going down to the beach. Coming?'

'No. I've got two pupils but first . . . is Dirk there?' Gillian asked. She spoke stiffly in a way unlike her, Peter thought.

Had she too, heard the absurd story of how he had broken beautiful Lucille's heart?

'I heard him arrive last night but haven't heard anything this morning, but then he always sleeps late . . .'

Gillian nodded, 'Yes, he's a night bird, he told me.'

'Want me to give him a message? I'm going up to change.'

'No, thanks. I'll go up myself later,' Gillian said as she turned away.

Peter went up to his cottage, changed and

hurried down to the beach. He had a favourite place, sheltered from the wind by a huge rock that looked like an unevenly-carved lion, but in the sunshine. He stretched out on the warm sand and closed his eyes. At least Lucille had gone, he thought happily.

It was rather strange, he realized later, but he didn't see either Gillian or Dirk again that day. He only realized it when he went to bed that night, later after a long bridge session at the Oswalds. He liked them for they played without anger and the evening had been very pleasant. Or rather would have been, if they hadn't talked constantly about their daughter, Lyndy. They were so convinced that she was a natural genius, so worried lest they be wrong, so upset because she was getting bad reports, and was still talking to her invisible friends. Peter had found it hard not to tell them there was nothing to worry about, that the girl of ten was still a child and would grow out of it and that what she needed most of all was a baby brother or sister!

'She was so good at French and now ...' Jock Oswald had sighed. 'The talk I had last week with her headmistress really upset me. It's as if Lyndy is deliberately trying not to use her brains. As if she is deliberately putting a block there.'

And Gwen, his wife, had looked annoyed. 'I have always said that if you have a talent, you must use it. Lyndy has but she won't. They said she had a wonderful aptitude for languages, but now ... I really don't know what to do, Peter. Maybe a different school ... ?'

Plumping up his pillow and turning it over for it was a hot night, Peter suddenly had an idea. He leapt out of bed, switched on the light and went to the kitchen where he always kept a pile of old newspapers. It took some time to find the article he wanted and when he read it, he glanced at the date on the paper. Was it too late?

Maybe if he went over in the morning ...

At that moment, he heard the roar of Dirk's scooter. It was three a.m. Unlike him to be so late, Peter thought, and went back to bed, to fall immediately into a deep sleep.

That night he dined with the Yeltons. When he arrived, Gillian was putting on a white linen coat over a white sheath frock.

'I've got a date, Peter, I know you won't mind ...' she said with a quick smile.

Her mother was almost embarrassingly apologetic.

'Most unlike Gillian. I can't think what's got into her these last few days. She's been so difficult. Last night for instance—she wasn't home until three a.m. Three a.m. Peter, I ask you. There are limits.'

Peter murmured sympathetically. So that explained Dirk's late return home! Was Gillian going out with Dirk tonight, too, he wondered. He felt a little worried. Dirk was a bit of a

144

mystery. People in the village often talked of it for he only arrived or left after dark, never had visitors or any mail. Certainly as he only came for week-ends, that could explain the mail, but all the same!

Gillian was young, the vulnerable age, and sorry for Dirk. However, that was Gillian and her parents' business, not his, he reminded himself, and the evening passed pleasantly. It was midnight when he left and Gillian had still not returned.

Her mother showed her anxiety. 'I'm not happy about Dirk. I do hope she isn't getting mixed up with a bad lot. There are two girls who always come down about now for a few weeks. Pauline and Heather. Very odd girls. What Gillian calls hippies. Broken homes, I gather, and they do just what they like. They rent a tiny flat on the front and ... well, of course, I know how some people gossip here but all the same, there's never smoke without fire ...'

'I can't imagine Gillian getting mixed up with them,' Peter said reassuringly. 'She's a very sensible girl.'

'That's what I thought but she seems to be changing,' Mrs. Yelton said worriedly.

Peter drove home thoughtfully for Mrs. Yelton's words had described his feelings. Gillian *had* changed.

The next day he called at the Oswald's. Lyndy was alone in the garden, the housekeeper was in the house, she said.

'Mind if I sit out here with you?' Peter asked casually.

Lyndy a long-legged thin girl, looked surprised. 'I don't mind, and nor does Richard.' She turned and looked at the ground. 'You don't mind, Richard?' then looked at Peter, 'no, he doesn't mind.'

'Thanks, mind if I smoke?' Peter asked as he sat down on the grass.

'Course not. Daddy smokes. Richard doesn't. He's too young yet. One day he will. One day he'll be a man and he's going to be the cleverest man in the world.'

'Is he, now?' Peter asked, keeping his voice casual. 'That's interesting. What's he going to be?'

'A scientist, of course. And I'm going to be very very proud of him. He's very very clever you know. Very very clever.'

'I'm sure he is . . . tell me, Lyndy, is he any good at French?'

He saw the wariness on her face. 'French?'

'Yes, only I have a problem and I thought maybe Richard could help me . . .'

Lyndy looked startled, as if it was the first time any grown up had accepted the existence of 'Richard'.

'What d'you want him to do?'

Peter looked away, pretending to study his pipe.

'A friend of mine has a dog. It's a poodle. A

146

little one. A friendly little dog but going to be very unhappy. His name is Gaston, and his mistress is French. Unfortunately she has been very ill and has to go to hospital and then abroad. She has to find a home for Gaston. But ... and this is where I wondered if Richard could help, Gaston can only understand French. You see, Gaston needs a new master or mistress but he doesn't know what you're talking about if you speak English. His mistress had some friends look after him who knew no French and poor little Gaston was miserable. He just sat and sat and he's really a very obedient little dog.'

Lyndy's face had lost its wary look. 'You want Richard to have the dog?' Her eyes brightened. 'But would Dad let me?'

'I don't see why not. A poodle isn't much trouble, he's house trained and, as I say, obedient, provided you can speak French, I mean if Richard would speak French to him.'

Lyndy had long fair hair, neatly done in two plaits. Now she sucked the end of one.

'I could help Richard with his French,' she said thoughtfully. 'I've got a book . . .'

'Well,' Peter stood up. 'Think about it and if your parents agree, why not come over with me tomorrow in my car and meet Gaston, he's a cute little dog. Bring Richard, too, of course, my car is big.'

'D'you really think Dad would let me have Gaston?' Lyndy asked eagerly. Peter noted that this time there was no mention of Richard.

'I'm sure he would,' Peter promised. He had already planned what he was going to say to Lyndy's parents. The child needed someone to love and care for—the little lonely language-blocked poodle was surely the answer. 'I'll come in about six o'clock to see your father.'

Lyndy went with him to the gate. 'I'll get my French book out and look up the words. What sort of things should I know?'

'Well ... things like Come here ... Sit down ... Naughty boy or That's a good boy ... but I think Gaston would like to be talked to, too. I mean, he's not just a dog, he's like a child, he needs a lot of love ...'

Lyndy gave a little skip. 'Oh I do hope Gaston loves me ...'

Peter smiled at her. 'I'm sure he will,' he said.

CHAPTER THIRTEEN

The weeks passed and the month of August drew nearer and as the mass of holiday makers grew, even Peter's quiet beach was crowded. On a very hot Sunday with the sea far out and seemingly miles of wet sand on which the children could race, Peter lay in his favourite position by the rocks. Round him there was no longer peace, instead children squabbling, or crying, shouting and laughing, mothers scolding, and Dads talking wistfully of cold beers.

Peter was startled when Gillian appeared for she seldom joined him now.

She sat down by his side. 'Have you seen Dirk? He's not in his cottage.'

'I didn't hear him go out,' Peter said stiffly.

During the last weeks Gillian had indeeed changed. She looked older, much less happy, and there was a restrained look about her that worried him. As if she had some secret she was determined to keep, no matter what it cost her.

She and Dirk had become inseparable during the weekends. Her mother had become more and more anxious, and Peter had gathered from hints dropped that there had been quarrels in the family about it. Everyone in the neighbourhood was talking about the pity of it—such a nice girl in love with a creature like Dirk!

Not that Peter had anything against Dirk. His appearance perhaps, but that was merely a sign of extreme youth. Certainly Dirk rather overdid it, but he wasn't bad. Most certainly not.

'I was talking to the Oswalds,' Gillian went on, twisting her fingers together, looking at them intently. She wore a white towelling coat over her matching bikini.

'They are so pleased about Lyndy. She is a different girl, thanks to you.'

'Thanks to Gaston.'

Gillian smiled. 'But you found Gaston for her.'

'Actually it was in reverse. I read about Gaston in the paper and realized it would help the three of them, Gaston, his mistress and Lyndy. It's amazing how that little dog loves her.'

'Richard seems to have vanished completely.'

'I knew he would. She needed someone to love . . .'

'Don't we all,' Gillian said, her voice sad.

'Gillian . . . you can't be . . . you can't be in love with Dirk,' Peter began.

Gillian turned to look at him. 'And why can't I?' she asked, her voice hostile. 'Because I am a sweet child?'

He was puzzled. 'No, you're not a child. But . . . but Dirk is wrong for you.'

'How d'you know?'

'Well, look, Gillian, let's be honest. What do we or anyone know about Dirk. Has he parents? Where does he live? What work does he do? Can you answer any of those questions?'

She shook her head, her mouth firmly closed, so Peter went on: 'He's a mystery. Why does he only arrive and leave after dark? Why does he have no visitors, no letters?'

Gillian gave a strange smile. 'I might ask that of you. At least I know you have no parents but I don't know where you live, or what work you do. You have no visitors—except Lucille that time—and no mail. What's the difference?'

'Between me and Dirk?' Peter began and chanced to turn his head. 'Look Gillian, the tide's coming in unusually fast.'

Gillian looked over the low group of rocks. 'It *is* coming in fast ...' She jumped to her feet. 'It's all right down here for this is all flat but it's by that headland. There is a flag warning them but few people notice it. Oh, look Peter ... those two kids ...' her voice rose in horror.

Peter was on his feet, staring at where the headland went out to the sea with an ugly cluster of rocks round which the sea twisted at high tide in savage currents. He could see the two children, a boy and a small girl, fishing in a pool, their backs to the waves that came racing towards them.

Peter began to run, Gillian was close behind him, both shouting at the children to run ashore. It was a race between them and the waves, and the waves were winning easily. As the water enveloped the two children, Gillian cried out:

'Look—there's Dirk ...'

Running down the headland was Dirk, jumping into the sea with a splash.

151

'But he can't swim . . .' Peter shouted. It had been one of the puzzling things about Dirk. He sunbathed, but never went into the water. He seemed almost scared of it.

Peter rushed into the water, scrambling his way over the half-covered rocks, swimming as the water got deeper. Now he could see that the boy was clinging to the rocks, the waves beating against him. Dirk already had the little girl in his arms and was obviously battling . . .

At last, swept out by the current Peter grabbed the boy, who clung to him, frightened, blood running down the side of his face. Peter was startled at the depth of the water already, at the way the waves whirled and tugged at him, pulling him back so that for every three strokes forward he seemed to be retreating two!

Gillian had run out to meet Dirk, staring at him unbelievingly. What had happened to his shoulder length frizzy hair? Now it was short and a different colour but she forgot it as she took the little girl in her arms and carried her ashore while Dirk, coughing and spluttering, stumbled after her, collapsing on the sand, and leaning forward to vomit.

'I thought you couldn't swim.'

Dirk gazed at her blankly. 'I can—when I have to but I hate it . . .'

The little girl was coughing and spluttering, too, as well as crying 'Mummy . . . Mummy . . .' but she seemed all right. Gillian looked out at the waves that came pounding towards them and saw Peter come ashore, stumbling over the rocks, carrying the boy in his arms.

'We'd better get a doctor . . .' she said as she saw the trickle of blood on the boy's face.

Peter was laying the boy on the ground gently.

'No need,' Peter said curtly. 'I am a doctor.'

'You are?' Gillian gasped and sat silently as she watched Peter quickly examine the boy and then the little girl.

He straightened. 'I think we should get them to hospital though they seem all right.'

Dirk stood up slowly. 'I'll go and phone for the ambulance.'

Peter stared at him, his face startled. 'Dirk . . .' he began and paused. Then he glanced at Gillian who gave a tiny shrug.

Seeming to understand, Dirk ran his hand over his short cropped hair and grinned. 'Oh, my wig you mean. It doesn't matter. I can always buy another.'

He hurried up the beach towards the caravan encampment where he knew there were several public call boxes. Meanwhile the crowd, losing interest when they saw the children were all right, drifted away.

Gillian held the little girl, with fair hair and dark blue eyes in her arms. 'We'll find your Mummy,' she promised and then looked at Peter who was leaning over the boy, who looked about seven with sandy coloured hair, his face white with fright.

'Mum had a headache and I said I'd look after Jenny. Mum's going to be mad at me . . .' his voice was uneven.

'Of course she won't be,' Gillian said quickly. 'How were you to know the tide came in so fast. Where d'you live?'

'We've got the fifth caravan on the right, the first row . . .'

'I see. I'll just wait until the ambulance gets here and then I'll go and tell her,' Gillian promised.

'You can tell her I think they're both fine. It's just that I'd like to make sure. Both have had a nasty shock,' Peter said. 'Something should be done about this dangerous part of the coast . . .' he spoke angrily and then stopped himself as if he wanted to say more. 'I'll see to it . . .' he finished, obviously making an effort to control himself. He managed a smile. 'Well, Gillian, two mysteries have been solved. Who I really am . . . and Dirk's ghastly hair! I wonder why he wore a wig. He isn't bald.'

'Why didn't you say you were a doctor?' Gillian asked. 'It isn't something to be ashamed of . . .'

They heard the screech of the ambulance in the distance and Peter gave a wry grin. 'It's a long story. Some other time.'

Gillian stood up, helping the little girl to her feet, smiling down at her. 'Now not to worry,

154

love. I'll go and get your Mummy and we'll probably be at the hospital as soon as you are . . .'

The child clung to her. 'You promise?'

'I promise.'

Peter took the little girl's hand. 'Gillian can go right away, Jenny, you'll be all right with me and . . . ?'

'Bobby . . .' the boy said. 'My head hurts.'

'We'll soon put that right.'

Gillian scrambled up the beach, past the groups of children and people, playing, reading, sleeping, in the sunshine. She saw the lines of caravans and tried to remember what Bobby had said.

'The fifth caravan on the right.'

Carefully she counted them and knocked on the closed door. There was no answer so she knocked again, louder this time. After all if the poor woman had had a headache she might be asleep.

The door of the next caravan opened and an elderly woman with her hair in curlers looked out.

'Mrs. Harrison's gone.'

Gillian turned to her. 'Maybe I'm at the wrong caravan. Has she two children, Bobby and Jenny?'

The tired-looking woman nodded. 'That's her all right. She went off with her suitcases and all. Said she couldn't stand it another moment.'

Gillian caught her breath with dismay. 'But the children?'

'She told me she was taking the cases to the coach stop, and then picking up the kids.' The old face wrinkled into lines of anxiety. 'Something happened to the kids?'

'No, luckily it hasn't but they were nearly drowned. They've gone to the hospital for a check-up. I have to find their mother. Perhaps she's looking for them on the beach.'

'That's queer, that is ...' the old woman said. 'Just a mo.' She vanished inside the caravan and then appeared, holding a piece of paper in her hand and coming down the steps. She had an apron tied round her waist and a grey cardigan over her shoulders.

'Just looked up the coach times. Mrs. Harrison went off about an hour ago and the coach'd have gone by now ...'

'But she hadn't picked up the children ...' Gillian began.

Another woman came from the caravan. A tall woman with her plaited red hair pinned round her head.

'I always said she was no good, that Marjorie Harrison ...'

She came down the steps wearing a smart green suit. 'Didn't I, Mother? No good, that's what she is, I said. Always leaving the kids on their own. I wouldn't mind betting you she's deserted 'em.'

'Oh no ...' Gillian said in dismay.

'You never did like her, Joannie. That was a wicked thing to say. She was a good mother but she was young and you couldn't blame her for wanting a bit of fun . . .' the older woman scolded.

'Where is the coach stop?' Gillian asked.

They told her and were still arguing about Mrs. Harrison as Gillian left them hurriedly.

Then she saw that the ambulance had come this side of the hill. Dirk must have told the hospital exactly where the near-tragedy had happened. Peter was standing by the door of the ambulance, speaking to the driver.

Gillian began to run towards him, waving her hand frantically. Somehow she had a feeling that Peter would know what to do— that if only Peter would see her . . . everything would be all right.

CHAPTER FOURTEEN

Sitting by the bedside of little Jenny, holding her hand tightly, and constantly telling her that Mummy would soon be there, Gillian kept wondering what Peter was doing.

It was wonderful the way he had immediately grasped the situation. He had seen her, hurried to meet her, listened to her breathless story, nodded understandingly and said, almost curtly:

'I'll cope. You go with the children. Tell them their Mummy is asleep but will soon be with them.'

'But how will you find her . . . ?' Gillian had cried, and she thought she would never forget the look on his face as he smiled reassuringly:

'Don't worry, I will.'

So she had got into the ambulance with the children, told them that their Mummy was sound asleep. Somehow it didn't seem to surprise them for Bobby said that his Mummy often slept and slept and they just couldn't wake her. Maybe, Gillian was thinking worriedly, their mother took drugs. Poor little things . . .'

She had explained to the doctor what Peter had told her to say and he had nodded understandingly and must have given the children sedatives for both were sleeping peacefully, Bobby's nasty graze hidden under a bandage. Now Gillian waited, wondering if Peter would find the children's mother—suppose she refused to come back with him? Would the poor kids have to go into an orphanage? Maybe they'd be found foster parents. Where was the father?

Dr. Armitage came to her. 'You needn't stay, Miss Yelton. The children are perfectly all right.'

Gillian smiled sheepishly. 'I know but . . .'

He nodded. 'You feel responsible until their mother comes. I understand. I'd suggest you

158

go and get something to eat and then come back. There's a nice little restaurant called The Blue Birds, just round the corner. The children won't wake up I promise you.'

Gillian stood up. 'All right ... if ... if Dr. Richardson,' how funny it sounded, she thought. 'If he comes here, will you tell him where I am?'

'Of course.'

When she went outside everything seemed changed. The sun had vanished and a sudden storm was brewing. The threatening clouds were low and menacingly dark. There was a chill breeze.

She hurried to the restaurant and realized she wasn't hungry. However, she ordered an omelette and sat near the huge window, gazing out at the dreary scene. Depression filled her as she thought of the two little kids. What sort of mother was it that could walk out like that? But if she was a drug addict maybe she was too far gone to reason sensibly. How terrible to have a mother like that.

How lucky she was, Gillian thought with a sense of shock for she had never thought of it before, to have such loving and understanding parents and realized with shame how bad-tempered she had been lately. The truth was she hated pretending she was in love with Dirk, for she most certainly wasn't. She was sorry for him but that was a different matter. She had deliberately let everyone think she was involved in order to kill the gossip that she was chasing Peter.

Had she chased him she wondered, without meaning to? For she had certainly not been in love with him, then.

Then?

She caught her breath and at that moment the skies seemed to open and the rain poured down. Pitiless, the water was bouncing up from the road surface, turning everything grey and miserable. Exactly as she felt. It couldn't be true . . . She must be imagining it . . .

But she wasn't.

And it was the truth.

She loved Peter Richardson. Dr. Peter Richardson as she now knew he was. Peter, who had known beautiful Lucille for many years, who loved her dearly, and was—at the moment—unable to marry her.

Oh no . . . Gillian cried out silently. That way there can only be heartache.

But it was too late. She knew she loved him. This terrible aching desolation that filled her as she accepted the fact made her realize that it was the truth. She loved a man who loved another—who saw her only as a 'sweet child'. Could anything be more painful?

How was she going to hide it? Wouldn't her eyes betray the secret that must be kept? Not only from Peter, but from her mother and the villagers too. Somehow or other, Gillian knew she must hide it. But how?

Her feet dragged as she went back to the hospital. Maybe she could go home and avoid meeting Peter? But it would only be a postponement and he might wonder why she had hurried away.

The children were awake when she reached the hospital and their mother was there, weeping and hugging them. A scrap of a girl, very thin, with enormous dark eyes and thick black hair. A girl who would have been very pretty but for the unhappiness in her face, the way the corners of her mouth were pulled down.

'Of course I'm not angry, Bobby boy . . .' she was saying as she hugged the boy, and then bent and kissed Jenny who clung to her. 'I ought to have found out about that dangerous place.'

Peter was standing by the bedside. He smiled at Gillian.

'You found . . .' Gillian began.

He nodded and put his finger to his mouth warningly.

'Mrs. Harrison, this is Miss Yelton who helped us rescue the children . . .' Peter said.

The unhappy looking girl turned her head and stared at Gillian. 'I don't know how to thank you . . .' she said, her voice thickening, her eyes filled with tears.

'I'm only glad we saw them,' Gillian said.

Peter drew her on one side.

'Gillian, I'll handle this. You can go home.'

She stared at him, startled and hurt by his curtness. After all, she was in this as much as he was. But maybe it was a good thing for it gave her a chance to escape.

She looked away quickly, suddenly wondering if he could read the message in her eyes. 'All right, Peter, I'm glad you found her.'

'I'll see you tonight . . .' he said.

'I may not be in . . .'

'Have you forgotten I'm coming to dinner? You asked me yourself.'

She swung round, startled. 'Did I? No, I couldn't have. It's the week-end.'

'Oh Dirk, I see. Well, I shouldn't think he'd have the nerve to put in an appearance after losing his wig.'

She glared at him for a moment. Now he was being smug.

'Is that worse than pretending to be someone you're not?'

'I didn't pretend to be anyone.'

'Oh yes you did. You pretended to be no one.' It helped her to feel angry with him, helped ease some of the pain.

He was smiling. 'So a doctor is a someone.'

'Of course he is . . .' she began and stopped because of the amusement on his face. She felt the colour flood her cheeks.

'Goodbye . . .' she said abruptly and walked out of the ward.

She caught a train to Cudjack and a bus to the village from there. Back at home, she

162

showered and dressed. Her parents had just come back from bowls.

'Peter's coming to dinner, Gillian,' her mother said, smiling at her. 'You haven't forgotten?'

Gillian hesitated. 'Did I ask him, Mum?'

Her mother nodded. 'Yes. We were discussing a T.V. programme we watch each week and he said he hadn't seen it and you said he must for it was really good—and you asked him for dinner tonight.'

'But ... well, Saturday nights I always go out with Dirk.'

'Dirk ...' her father said and began to laugh. 'I hear he wears a wig. I always wondered how he'd managed to grow that dreadful mop.'

'Yes, Miss Owen was telling me. She saw him scuttling into his cottage as if scared stiff and his hair was cut short so he must have lost a wig ...' Gillian's mother said, chuckling. 'Honestly what you see in that ghastly creature.'

'He lost his wig saving a child's life,' Gillian said coldly. She opened the front door. 'He happens to be my friend so please don't be so beastly.'

She ignored their startled looks and slammed the door behind her. She walked up the hill towards the cottages. Poor Dirk. Now he'd be the laughing stock of the village.

When she reached the cottage, she saw with

163

relief that Dirk's scooter was still there. So he hadn't gone!

The front door was shut so she knocked on it.

'Who's that?' Dirk shouted.

'Me. Gill.'

The door opened and Dirk stood there. But a Dirk she had never seen before. He wore ordinary clothes—what her parents would have called 'normal' clothes. A pale grey suit, a white shirt, a dark blue silk tie.

'Why, Dirk . . .' Gillian said, not sure what to say or if to remark on the change in him.

He grinned. 'Come in, Gill. I'm making a cuppa. Like one?'

'Thanks.'

Curiously she looked round the room. She had never been in his cottage before. It was sparsely furnished with nothing beyond necessities, scrupulously clean and neat, piles of books on the floor. All very drab and colourless.

She followed him to the kitchen. He made the tea with the practised hand of a man used to managing for himself then turned and smiled.

'How are the kids?'

She told him and about their mother, and how Peter had somehow traced her.

'What a tragedy it might have been . . .' Dirk said, his face clouding. 'It nearly happened to me, once, Gill. I was about seven or eight, swept away by a current and just rescued in time. I was unlucky, though, for I was badly battered about and in hospital for some months. I've never forgotten it. I'm petrified when my face goes under water. I can't seem to forget the horror of it all.'

'So that's why you never swim. I can understand. I hope Bobby won't feel like that.'

'I doubt it. Peter got to him in time. I'm glad the mother turned up, though. She sounds as though she takes drugs.'

'That's what I thought. Dirk, I was so sorry for her. She's young. Can't be much more than twenty-four and she looks ghastly and lovely, too, if you know what I mean.'

'Maybe her husband's walked out on her ... maybe she hasn't one. Another cup?' Dirk asked. Then he grinned: 'Well, aren't you going to ask me why I wore a wig? Why such extraordinary clothes? For a girl, you're very uninterested.'

Gillian smiled. She liked this Dirk much better than the other one. 'I am interested but it is your business, not mine. Weren't you surprised to learn Peter was a doctor?'

'No. Remember what I told you about the first time he and I really talked? That I had a feeling he was sorry for me and felt I had no future. Did I shock him very much?'

'Not shock him, just puzzle him. He thought you were a sort of Jekyll and Hyde, two people.'

'Very bright of our medical friend.' Dirk laughed. 'He's right. I am two people. Want to know why?'

'Of course.'

'Good. Relax for it's a long story.'

It was a long story and a tragic one. Dirk, orphaned as a child, was brought up by strict but loving grandparents.

'Both are perfectionists. Nothing but the best is good enough. I was always in trouble at first and then I discovered how to make them happy. They were kind, you see. Generous too. And they made lots of sacrifices for me. They weren't rich but I could have everything I wanted. If it was good for me. Or ...' he smiled suddenly, 'if they thought it was good for me! I had a good education and soon learned that they were proud of me. I was grateful for all they'd done so I had to succeed at everything. It was unutterably boring and not my idea of living so I took refuge in a world of fantasy. I used to imagine all the things I'd like to do and couldn't and, in a way, it helped me. But as I grew older ...'

'Dirk, how old are you, really?' Gillian interrupted.

He grinned. 'Just seventeen.'

'I thought you were younger than you said.'

He laughed. 'I'm seventeen at home and twenty here. Can I go on?'

'Sorry. Please do.'

'Well, I managed to persuade the old folk

that I needed somewhere at the week-ends that was quiet where I could study uninterrupted yet be able to keep healthy by swimming and going for long walks. A friend of theirs had this cottage and wanted to get rid of it so they bought it and furnished it for my week-ends. They respect my need to be alone to study and—frankly—I think they enjoy their week-ends without me around to worry about . . .

'I can wear the grooviest clothes, play the hottest music, do all the things I couldn't do at home. Oh, I suppose I could do them but it would upset the poor darlings and they do feel so responsible for me.'

'You study here?'

'And how. Peter thinks I sleep late as he doesn't hear me moving around or with the radio on. I get up every day at six and work like mad. I've got to work to keep the old dears happy . . .'

'Dirk . . .' Gillian was dismayed to find her eyes full of tears. 'I think you're a darling. It's wonderful of you.'

'Why? They've been good to me so why shouldn't I be good to them. Unfortunately I think I was seen today . . .'

'Yes. Miss Allen.'

'It's already spread around? Oh, hell! Only if someone recognized me and told the old dears what I did, they'd be awfully hurt. They'd feel they'd denied me something—that they ought to have let me dress as I liked.'

'D'you really like dressing like that?'

He grinned. 'It's fun, sometimes. I'm so used to playing the good little boy, that I like to shock people.'

'That explains why you deliberately shock poor old Nanny.'

'Exactly. She does remind me of Gran. Anyhow I'll be on my way after dark tonight and you won't be seeing me for a while. I may be back later on, though. I love it here.'

'I'll miss you, Dirk.'

'I'll miss you too, Gill. It's been great knowing you.'

'I'd better go. Peter is supposed to be coming to dinner.'

He went with her to the door but didn't go outside.

'You won't split on me? My age and all that, I mean.'

She smiled at him. 'Trust me.'

'I do.'

He closed the door quietly as she walked down the paved path to the little white gate.

She was startled as she went down the hill to see Peter in his doorway.

'Hullo . . .' he said and he sounded annoyed. 'I called in at your house to report on proceedings and found you were out.'

'I thought you weren't coming until tonight.'

'I suppose you couldn't wait to see Dirk. Well, solved the problem? Why does he wear a wig?'

Gillian looked at the tall, once too-thin man whose face when she first saw it had been strained and drawn, whose mouth had drooped, whose eyes had been unhappy, and she thought how different that first man was from the man standing before her now. He had put on weight, his skin was brown from sea breezes, he looked happy, relaxed and very sure of himself. Pendennis had done a lot for Peter Richardson—Dr. Richardson. But so had Peter, for Pendennis.

'I'll tell you tonight. I must see to the horses.'

'I'll walk home with you. I feel restless.'

'All right,' she hesitated. 'What's happening to the children?'

'They're spending the night in the hospital and Mrs. Harrison is fixed up in town and then they're going back to the caravan.'

'How on earth did you find her?'

He shrugged. 'Not hard. I found out which coach she'd gone on, phoned a message through to the next stop, got her to call back and told her what had happened. Three months ago her husband walked out on them. They had already booked and paid in advance for the caravan but her money was getting less and less. She's been taking drugs in a mild way to boost her morale—that was how she put it. I gathered she loves her husband dearly and is terribly hurt by his behaviour—and I think

169

she—well, she just couldn't take any more. She knew the children would be cared for. Personally I think she had suicide in mind.'

'Poor girl. She looks so young.'

'Yes. She was married at seventeen and has had a bad deal but she goes on loving the man. I can't understand it.'

Gillian turned her head. 'Can't understand what?'

'How anyone can love someone who is cruel to them.'

She smiled wryly. 'But you can't understand love at all, can you?'

That was what he had implied yet he was hopelessly in love with Lucille. Why couldn't he be honest and admit that he loved someone who was not, for some reason or another, available?

'I think she'll be all right, now,' he said, ignoring her remark. 'I've given her my partner's address, he's very good at helping people who dabble in drugs and also an introduction to a firm who welcomes workers with small children, they even have a nursery school attached to the factory. One of the few firms with such sensible views.'

They were at the Yeltons' gate now.

'Can I help you with the horses?' Peter asked.

Gillian looked at him quickly and then away. Why had he suggested that? she wondered.

'No thanks, I'll see you later ...' she said curtly.

He hesitated. 'Did Dirk tell you why he wore a wig?'

Gillian drew a long deep breath. 'Yes he did and while it's no business of yours or anyone else's, I'll tell you he did it for kicks. During the week he's a very conservative bowler-hat-and-umbrella type and it relaxes him to pretend at week-ends to be a hippie. Not a very thrilling reason, is it? Sorry, if I've disappointed you ...' Gillian said nastily and suddenly wanted to cry. Why was she like this? Why did she want to hurt Peter?

She hurried through the gate, not looking back, not even looking forward very well for her eyes were full of tears and she was glad when the dogs came racing to greet her, noisy with their warm welcome. At least, they loved her.

CHAPTER FIFTEEN

There was no doubt, Peter decided, but that Gillian was in love with Dirk. The way she had snubbed him when he offered to help her with the horses because she looked tired, it was obvious that his remarks about Dirk had offended her.

A strange story of hers. How much of it

could be true? He couldn't see Dirk as a bowler-hat-and-umbrella type. The idea was fantastic . . .

Walking back to Puffin Cottage, Peter had debated in his mind as to whether he should call in at Dirk's. After all, he might want to know how the children were. On the other hand, it might be wiser to wait for Dirk to call on *him*, Peter decided so he went into his own cottage, had a quick bath and got ready for dinner at the Yeltons.

Dirk's cottage was quiet and when Peter set off down the hill just before seven o'clock, he saw Dirk's scooter parked outside. The door and windows of the cottage were closed, which was unusual. Peter hesitated. Could Dirk be ill? he wondered. Had he hurt himself when he dived into the water, bravely—if foolishly—ignoring the danger of the rocks? He'd undoubtedly saved the girl's life. Had he been injured in the process?

Somehow the closed windows and door denied this possibility. It looked more as if Dirk wanted to be alone. Perhaps someone had laughed at him about his missing wig? In the end, Peter decided to do nothing until the next morning. In any case, there was always the chance that Dirk might turn up for dinner, if Gillian had invited him. Without his wig? Peter found himself grinning, imagining how the Yeltons would tease the boy. For *boy* he still was in Peter's eyes and imagining Dirk as

172

an umbrella-and-bowler-hatted man was quite impossible.

Dirk was not at the Yeltons'. Nor was Gillian. Her mother apologized profusely and said that Gillian had said she felt ill. 'So I sent her to bed, Peter. I think this afternoon was a nasty shock. I mean, those children could have drowned.'

'I know. If we hadn't ... or rather, if Gillian hadn't noticed the way the tide was racing in, we'd never have got there in time. Dirk was on the headland, he'd have got the little girl, but I doubt if Bobby could have clung to the rocks much longer. His fingers were all cut and raw, poor kid. There should be a means of preventing people from paddling in that area.'

'There should,' Gillian's father agreed gravely. 'The matter has often been brought up but they always postpone it. So far no one has died as a result. I think they've been waiting for proof that it *is* dangerous. They say people should stay away where there are those flags that say it is dangerous.'

'Small children don't know what the flags mean. Something should be done about it,' Peter said irritably.

Yelton nodded. 'I couldn't agree more but I tell you, Peter, it's like banging your head against a brick wall to get anything done here. They always postpone it, will consider it ... that's sort of codwash.'

'I see ...' Peter hesitated. 'Gillian's in bed?'

'Yes, I gave her a sleeping pill and she's sound asleep. She seemed very upset about the children's mother. Quite a girl, she said . . .'

'Yes, a very sad case . . .' Peter told them all about it but as he talked, he found himself wondering if Gillian *was* upstairs, or if she had sneaked out of the house and was, at that moment, with Dirk. Yet there was no means of finding out.

In any case, he told himself crossly, it was none of his business. Gillian was no child. She was twenty years old and should be able to manage her own affairs. If only she wasn't so sentimental, mixing up sympathy with love and getting the two things confused.

When Peter walked home, there was a bright moon. The first thing he noticed as he glanced up at the cottage above his, was that Dirk's scooter had gone. That meant, then, that Dirk was all right and there was nothing to worry about so he went to bed without any anxiety for the wigless lad.

It was raining hard next day and a dismal outlook from his front door as Peter stood, hands thrust deep into his trouser pockets, and gazed at the grey expanse and the swirling ugly waters. Glancing curiously up towards Dirk's cottage, he caught his breath.

The scooter was not there.

Where had Dirk spent the night? It was the first time Dirk had ever spent one of the week-end nights away. Well, he'd be back later,

Peter decided, and went to light a fire for it wasn't actually cold but one of those cheerless miserable days.

The quietness seemed to hit him. He was so used to the ceaseless roar on the sea that he hardly noticed that but normally at week-ends he would hear the blare of Dirk's radio. Suddenly he felt uneasy, found his wellingtons, mackintosh and a weird-looking sou'wester he'd bought and went out into the windy wet day and up to Dirk's cottage.

He looked through the windows and saw that the piles of books had gone. Everything looked neat and empty. Dirk had gone. For good? Was he so sensitive that he could not face the teasing about his wig? Yet that was unlike Dirk. He had enjoyed arresting attention, having people talk about him.

Walking back to his cottage, Peter wondered if Dirk would be back the following week-end, having bought a new wig. Outside his front door he hesitated. The cottage was so quiet. The long empty day stretched ahead.

Glancing down the hill, he noticed the Norris's house. Maybe Fiona would like him to 'mother-sit' so she could pretend she was going to church and instead meet her boy friend. It would be something to do.

Fiona looked startled when she opened the door. He noticed her eyes were red-rimmed and her voice uneven as she asked him in.

'I thought I might get a nice cup of tea

here,' he joked.

She smiled gratefully. 'Mother will be thrilled. We've just heard that you're a doctor.'

Of course! Peter had forgotten that! Now everyone would know. Well, it didn't really matter. 'That's right.' He smiled. 'I wondered if you'd like to go to church. I know you don't often get the chance and I'll look after your mother . . .'

She smiled at him, her whole face lighting up and then her mouth trembled and he saw the tears fill her eyes.

'Ken says I must make a choice . . .' she whispered, leaning forward towards Peter. 'He . . . he threatens to go away. He says . . . he says he can't wait for ever. But she needs me, doesn't she? I can't just walk out but . . .'

Peter put his hand on her arm. 'We'll find a way,' he said softly. 'Ask Ken to be patient a little longer.'

Fiona's eyes widened with eager excitement. 'You've thought of something?'

'I think so.'

She surprised him as she leant forward and kissed him lightly and then turned away. 'Mother,' she called out. 'You have a visitor. Dr. Richardson. Would you like to go in, Peter? I'll make us some tea.' Her voice had changed completely—now it seemed to lilt with fresh hope.

Peter silently cursed himself. It was easy to promise things on an impulse and far harder to carry them out. What could he do to help this girl?

Mrs. Norris was patting her hair as he entered the room. She was sitting, huddled in a rug, in an arm-chair by the fire.

'How very nice of you to come, Dr. Richardson.'

'Peter please . . .' Peter said, smiling at her.

'Thank you. Peter . . .' She beamed happily. 'Fiona . . .' she called. 'Tea, please, and some of those nice chocolate biscuits. And we'd like it this morning and not tomorrow . . .' she added sharply.

'Now . . . now, Peter, do tell me all about it. You saved the children's lives.'

'We saved them,' Peter said patiently. 'Dirk, Gillian and I.'

'Dirk? Oh, you mean that scruffy layabout. Ugh . . . I've seen him walk down the road and he really gave me a headache. What his parents must think of him . . . That ghastly hair . . . oh, of course . . .' she laughed. 'I expect you've heard. It was just a wig. What sort of man is it wears a wig . . . ?'

Fiona came into the room carrying the heavy tray. It tilted and the cups and saucers slid forward and Peter, on his feet at once, just caught at the tray in time, straightened it and took it out of her hands.

'Really, Fiona,' her mother snapped. 'Surely you can carry a tray without dropping it. Peter, as a doctor, I ask your advice. What is the

177

matter with Fiona these days? Always dropping things, being clumsy, forgetting . . . I just don't know her at all. She's changed so much. Fiona—what are you thinking of? You've only brought two cups and saucers.'

Fiona stood in the doorway, turning, her face pale.

'I thought as . . . as Dr. Richardson was here, I'd go to church . . .'

'Well, really, that's not very hospitable of you. We might want some more tea . . .'

'It was my suggestion,' Peter said quietly. 'Fiona isn't getting enough fresh air and the walk to the church will do her good.' He nodded at the girl in the doorway. 'Don't hurry back, Fiona, we've a lot to talk about . . .'

The door closed and Mrs. Norris beamed. 'Yes, we always find so much to talk about, Peter. It's such a delight to me to meet an intelligent man like you. I feel such a prisoner here . . .'

Peter poured out the tea and handed Mrs. Norris a cup.

'I still feel you would be happier in a city.'

'I certainly would. I love London dearly and have lots of friends there but Fiona would hate it . . . I'd like to move but . . .'

Peter let Mrs. Norris talk on and on, occasionally putting in a word here and there; wondering how much was the truth, how much wishful thinking. Did Mrs. Norris honestly believe she was doing Fiona a good service by living in the country, absolutely dependent on the girl, turning her life into the equivalent of that of a prisoner? He wondered which was the best way to tackle the subject . . .

'You know, Mrs. Norris, I feel Fiona's clumsiness is due to ill-health.'

'Ill-health?' Mrs. Norris's voice was shocked. 'Is she ill?'

'Not yet but . . .' he paused, watching the face opposite him. She really looked concerned as she leaned forward.

'Please tell me the truth, Doctor.'

He smiled. 'Peter, please. Don't look so alarmed. It's largely a nervous condition. She is very concerned for you and lives under very tense conditions.'

'Concerned for me? There's nothing wrong with me . . .' Mrs. Norris began indignantly and stopped, her cheeks florid. 'I mean this arthritis makes it hard for me to get around and my heart is a bit . . . well, not what it used to be, but there's no need for Fiona to worry about me.'

'But I think you may have to worry about her.' He had heard the front door slam and knew Fiona was back. 'Encourage her to sit out in the sunshine, Mrs. Norris, make sure she eats well, plenty of fruit, and try—I know this takes courage but I'm sure you've got more than your share—try to let her see that you are not entirely dependent on her. You see . . .' he leaned down, speaking gently, 'one of the main reasons for this sort of tension is the feeling of responsibility for you that Fiona has. She *has* to keep well because you need her. She's worried stiff about what would happen to you if she wasn't here to look after you.'

'Why, nothing, of course,' Mrs. Norris sounded indignant. 'I can get around.'

'But who'd do the housework and the cooking?'

'Well . . . well . . . I could . . . I . . .'

'Maybe if Fiona saw that you could manage without her, some of her tenseness would go. It's a terrific strain to feel so . . . well, so necessary to another person.'

The door opened and Fiona stood there, her eyes sparkling.

'See what I mean, Mrs. Norris,' Peter said, taking the soft white hand of his hostess in his. 'Fiona looks better already for a little fresh air.'

Fiona saw him to the door. 'Well?' she whispered eagerly.

'First step taken. Make a great fuss of your mother, Fiona, let her see how much she means to you.'

'Oh, she does! That's what makes it all so difficult.'

He smiled. 'Don't worry. Everything'll work out all right.'

The rain had stopped and the sun had burst through the clouds that had drifted away.

Several boats had ventured out into the turbulent sea and there were quite a number of people about.

He saw the 'local gossips' coming towards him and looked round quickly to escape but he was too late.

'Dr. Richardson,' Miss Natalie Jones said, coming towards him, her voice coy as usual. 'You naughty young man not to tell us you were a doctor. It will be nice knowing you are. Our Dr. Walton is always busy so if there ever is an emergency may we call upon you?'

'Of course we can,' her companion said crossly. 'Dr. Richardson is a doctor and a doctor's duty is to anyone in need. Why didn't you tell us?'

It was the question he had been expecting. And quite simple to answer.

'I came here because I'd been overworking and was on the edge of a breakdown. I was advised not to mention the fact that I was a doctor in case . . .'

Miss Jones giggled: 'In case we all called on you! I certainly hope I have to—such a handsome young man . . .'

'Stop talking such nonsense, Natalie.' Miss Owen said crossly. 'And how long had you to stay here?'

'Six months.'

'A very long holiday!'

'What did happen to Mr. Thatcher's wig?' Natalie asked eagerly. 'We heard it came off in the sea. I wonder why he wore it—you'd think he'd have known that in the water it would come off.'

'I doubt if he had time to think. He saw these children were in danger of being drowned and jumped into the water. He saved the little girl's life . . .'

'And you saved the boy's,' Natalie said eagerly. 'Gillian told us how brave you were.'

'I don't think it was a question of courage,' Peter knew his voice was cold but the two old gossipers were getting on his nerves. 'One acts instinctively.'

'The children are all right?'

'Of course they're all right,' her companion said, 'Gillian told us that.'

'Excuse me . . .' Peter said and they stood aside politely to let him walk down the rest of the hill.

He walked aimlessly, glad of the sunshine and wishing he'd taken his wet mackintosh back to the cottage and changed out of the cumbersome wellingtons. Where was he going? Where was there to go?

'Doctor . . . doctor . . .' a shrill young voice screamed and Peter turned.

Mike Raines was racing down the hill, waving wildly. Peter waited, very conscious that the gossipers had heard Mike call and were standing there, watching and waiting to see what would be the outcome.

Mike's cheeks were bright red. 'I'm sorry I

didn't come yesterday, Doctor, but I had a cold and Mum said . . .'

Peter smiled. 'I understand.' Actually it had been a relief for sometimes he had to invent jobs for the boy to do!

'Mum saw you go by and wondered if you'd like to come to dinner today? We're having steak and kidney pie and blackberry and apple tart and Mum got some cream and . . .' Mike's hand went into Peter's. 'Come back now?' he asked wistfully, 'Can you play snap? And I've got a new car for my collection I want to show you . . .'

'Of course,' Peter said and hand in hand they walked past the two elderly ladies who pretended to be on their way, their heads together as they chatted.

Oh well! Peter thought. Who cares. They'll invent something to gossip about in any case, so what does it matter?

In a way it did matter, although Peter was not aware of this but Gillian heard so much gossip about Peter at times that she wondered if he was deliberately encouraging the gossipers in their favourite occupation. What with Mike and his pretty young widowed mother constantly asking Peter to a meal, there was talk of Jacquie with her family of brothers and sisters, who was obviously upset because her father was going to get married again. Jacquie had been seen out twice with the 'doctor' as Peter was now called by most of the locals. Then there were the letters that came three times a week from London. Mrs. Weir in the post office knew who they were from.

'I didn't look of course,' she always added, 'but Miss Harding puts her name and address on the back of the envelopes so I can't help knowing, can I? She's beautiful and really loves him so much. Else she wouldn't write so often, would she? I don't think he ever answers, the letters, the cold beast. Leastways he never buys any stamps from me.'

This all made it even more clear to Gillian that although he would probably deny it, Peter *was* in love with Lucille. The fact that he bought no stamps from Mrs. Weir meant nothing. He had once told Gillian how he hated the atmosphere in the local post office where there was a silence as soon as he entered the shop-cum-post-office and everyone looked at him, and he had a feeling that not only had he interrupted their discussion of him, but that the instant he left the shop, their tongues would start to wag again! He probably got enough stamps on his trips to Cudjack.

Peter was in love with Lucille. Just six simple words but they meant so much. Sometimes Gillian found herself longing to run away from home, to travel thousands of miles so that she need never see him again. It was funny how different real love was from the love you read

184

about in books. She had never expected to feel this ache, this sense of hopelessness because she loved someone who loved another. She had never thought being in love meant this breathlessness when she saw him, this embarrassing rush of tears to her eyes when she heard a tune like *'I could have danced all night'* *or* Engelbert Humperdinck sing *'I Danced the Last Waltz with You'*. The emotions raised by both tunes were so exactly what she felt. If only Peter had never come to Pendennis, if only she had never got involved with him . . .

Involved. That was Peter's word. He had admitted he didn't want to become involved because of the pain that was bound to follow. She had thought him a cynic. Yet that was how she felt, now. She was involved emotionally with Peter, although it was a one-sided involvement, and it did hurt! So he had been right. But what had made him fall in love with Lucille in the first place if she was unattainable? Gillian began to laugh. Wasn't that what she had done herself? She had known it was hopeless from the word go. She had believed then it was because Peter had no time for marriage—but he had told her plainly, hadn't he? Just as Peter had, she had done the most foolish thing imaginable—allowed herself to fall in love with someone who belonged to another. Allowed? She laughed at herself again but the tears were near. How did you stop yourself from falling in love?

It was a question to which she could find no answer. Although she avoided Peter as much as she could—and she had a feeling that he was avoiding her, too!—whenever she saw him she felt the adrenaline speeding through her veins, making her heart race, causing her to feel breathless and her legs weak.

A strange feeling, embarrassing, tragic in many ways for it only made her realize more and more the folly of it all. It was almost masochistic—as if she wanted to *hurt* herself. But in such a small enclosed community, it was impossible for them not to meet at times. Perhaps it was at those times she felt hurt the most—for Peter had returned to his kindly condescending attitude as if she was just a child—and that was the last thing she wanted to be in his eyes!

CHAPTER SIXTEEN

It was a hot September; what some call an *Indian summer*. Although many of the holiday makers had left, there were still quite a crowd on the beaches but Peter rarely went down there now he played tennis regularly as well as golf, and had even temporarily joined the bowls club. It took him out in the open air and gave him the chance to meet people.

Oddly enough, the one person he rarely met was Gillian. Sometimes he felt annoyed with her for she was behaving childishly. She had never forgiven him for what he said about Dirk—yet he had said nothing nasty, nothing unkind. Indeed he had liked Dirk.

In a way, the person he missed most was Dirk. Often on a Friday night, he would catch himself lying awake in bed, waiting for that familiar roar of his scooter. Dirk had never been back and now he had been forgotten. No one ever mentioned him. But had Gillian forgotten him? Peter was sure she had not!

Perhaps the most infuriating part of his life was the regular delivery, three times a week, of letters from Lucille. Sometimes there was nothing in the envelopes. Sometimes a few words. Never very much. Something like:

'I won't let you forget me.'

or

'I'm still here, waiting.'

Why must she pester him so much, he wondered. How did you get rid of such a nuisance?

It was all in Lucille's mind. There had never been any kind of relationship or, what she liked to call *affinity*, between them. They had met at the same cocktail and dinner parties and she was always ringing him to say she'd been given tickets for a concert and would he

187

join her, but he had always found a legitimate excuse. He did not like her, in fact, there were times when he disliked her. Yet she would hang on to him . . .

September came, the schools opened, the holiday-makers had dwindled away when the letter arrived.

Instantly Peter recognized his partner's handwriting.

'We're looking forward to seeing you. Only two weeks more and you'll be back in the rat race. Your stand-in was good but not you. There's plenty of work waiting. I expect you're counting the days. I only hope you haven't been too bored. By the way, your friend—if such she is—Lucille phoned me to check if this *was* the end of your six months' holiday. She is booking seats at the theatre and taking you out to dinner to celebrate your return on your first night back. She seemed very upset—says you never answer her letters. Frankly, old man, I think you were a fool to give her your address. She's like a leech and could be dangerous so, for heaven's sake, watch your step!'

Two weeks left! Was it possible that time had gone so swiftly? He went out into the sunlit world, the sea so serene, the waves racing in slowly and with a strange dignity.

He walked to the edge of the cliff and looked down at the rocks with the snow-white foam splashing over them. He drew several deep breaths, then turned and looked down the hill at the placid expensive houses in their neat little suburban backwater, at the cottages on the hillside, some enlarged, some rebuilt, a few as they were originally, his amongst that few.

This had been his home for six months. Months that had passed as fast as weeks usually do. Months that had begun seeming like years and yet had flown by in the end.

And why?

Because of Gillian.

He thrust his hands deep into his pockets and turned to face the sea, not seeing it. Seeing instead the elf-like face of Gillian, with her slanted green eyes, her quick warm smile, her short dark hair, the freckles on her nose. Gillian who had adopted him like the lame ducks she always helped. Gillian who had taught him how to meet people and like them, how to enjoy helping them solve apparently insolvable problems, who had opened up a whole new world in which he had learned to laugh and relax, to play games, to . . .

He frowned. No, that wasn't true. He liked her, that was all.

Yet lately she had dropped him, just like the proverbial hot potato. Oh, she was polite enough, even friendly in a stiff reserved way, but it was a long time since they had been alone, or had a private conversation. She was so engrossed in her beloved Dirk that she thought of no one else.

189

Two weeks more and then back to London. He shivered despite the warm sunshine. Could he bear to go back there?—to the screech of jet planes, the roar of the buses, the incessant noise of the cars, the mad scramble on the pavements, the unceasing row of patients waiting at the surgery, the long exhausting day in which you did everything to the best of your ability but like an automaton. There was nothing personal in that life, no . . . no . . .

Love. That was what Gillian would have said—in those early days when she had laid down the law about the necessity of loving your fellow creatures.

But how could you *love* someone for whom you could only spare a few moments because of the long line awaiting your attention? How could you *love* someone about whom you knew so little, perhaps the fact that they'd had mumps and German measles as a child and were now suffering from an ugly allergy? How could you *love* someone who was just a number on a card?

Could he bear to live in that white Regency house overlooking other houses and chimney pots? How could he leave the sea, the trees and the gorse?

He began to walk down the hill, taking long strides, head thrust forward almost aggressively, hands in his pockets, his face thoughtful. He had no choice. He was David's partner. David needed him, relied on him.

Maybe he could make changes. Get a house in the Green Belt. But how would he manage? That would mean a housekeeper and a gardener, and sleeping at his flat—for he'd have to keep that on—for the nights he was on duty. Would it work?

A small white poodle came racing up the hill, barking furiously and then running in circles round Peter as he recognized him. Peter bent and patted the little dog, looked up and saw Gwen Oswald walking towards him.

'Peter,' she said. 'We're so happy about Lyndy. This little Gaston has certainly done the trick.'

She smiled at him. 'She is a different child. She doesn't talk to her invisible friends any more . . . oh, and Peter . . .' she hesitated and laughed: 'I thought you'd like to know, Lyndy will be getting a baby brother or sister in about five months time.'

Peter smiled. 'I am glad, Gwen. Are you?'

Gwen nodded. 'Yes, and so is Jock.'

'You've told Lyndy?'

'Not yet. We thought we'd tell her as a birthday present. We shall miss you, Peter. Bye . . .' She called to the dog in French and they hurried down towards their house.

Peter, puzzled, followed more slowly. Why had she said goodbye? How had she known? Had Gillian kept count of the time? How had she known?

As he reached the level road, Gillian's dogs

came racing to meet him, Solak holding Peter's hand gently in his mouth. Gillian, in her riding clothes, came out of the gate, saw him, hesitated as if wanting to go back, and then came forward.

'Hullo, Peter . . .'

He stared at her. How she had changed. She looked years older, her face was tense, her eyes miserable. Her affair with Dirk wasn't making her happy.

'I'm leaving in two weeks.'

'Yes, I . . .' Gillian began and went red. 'I guessed it must have been about that. The six months have gone fast. But it's like that sometimes, isn't it. Sometimes time drags—at other times it goes terribly fast and you just don't know where you are . . .'

Puzzled, Peter listened. This wasn't like Gillian, gabbling away as if afraid to leave him time to question her. Why had she to talk such rubbish?

'I shall miss Pendennis,' he said when he got a chance.

Gillian turned her head away as if disinterested. 'Pendennis will miss you.'

'Pendennis has done me a lot of good.'

'You've done Pendennis a lot of good, too,' she said, still half-turned away.

He walked round to stand in front of her so that he could see her face. 'I don't see that. I've just lived here.'

He looked at her curiously—what was

upsetting her? She looked up at him, her eyes half-closed as if the sun was hurting them. 'Oh, Peter, don't be modest. You helped the Oswalds with Lyndy's problem, Mike Raines is a different child, Ginger never gets bullied these days, and look at Mrs. Norris. Up and about, doing her own housework, even talking of going to London to live. How do you do it?'

He frowned. 'I didn't *do* anything, actually. It just happened.'

Gillian gave an odd smile. 'Just a happening? Pity they don't happen more often and the world would be a much happier place. When are you going? Two weeks time? Mum and Dad will want to give you a farewell party . . .' she laughed. 'Don't frown like that. You can't get out of it, you know.'

He smiled. 'I know. I'm not even sure I want to.'

'You'll be glad to get back to your beloved London . . .'

'My beloved London?' he frowned. 'Now when have I ever called it that?'

He saw the colour fill her cheeks, saw the quick fear in her eyes before she turned away.

'I don't remember, sorry, I'm pretty busy. See you some time, Peter.'

'Yes . . .' he said thoughtfully, watching her as she hurried towards her stables, calling the dogs. 'See you some time.'

He walked slowly back to his cottage.

CHAPTER SEVENTEEN

The farewell party was given with Peter's friends crowding round him, insisting he came back to see them.

'You doctors should have more holidays,' Gwen Yelton said firmly. 'Remember there is always a spare bed waiting for you here.' She glanced quickly at Gillian who was talking to a girl friend. 'Peter, please keep in touch with us,' Gwen Yelton's voice was lowered. 'I think Gillian will grow out of it.'

'Grow out of it?' he asked puzzled but she shook her head and turned away as he found Gillian by his side.

'What was Mum talking about?'

'Oh, just . . . well, just . . .'

Gillian laughed. 'I know. Just! I don't suppose she will ever stop matchmaking until the day I marry.'

'You're going to be married?' Peter said, startled.

Gillian, looking unusually attractive in an amber-coloured silk frock smiled and shrugged her shoulders.

'Who knows. I told you that was my ambition, didn't I?'

'Yes, to marry and have four children.'

'And your ambition?' Gillian asked. 'Of course, your work. Well, Peter, it's been nice knowing you. You're off in the morning and I may not see you so I'll say goodbye now . . .' She held out her hand, stiffly.

Conscious of the people around him, talking in groups, moving round the room, Peter was puzzled.

'But the party isn't over, Gillian.'

'I know but I've a bad headache so am going to bed. Goodbye Peter . . .'

They shook hands solemnly and then she turned and almost ran out of the room. Peter stood still for a few moments, momentarily shocked. What on earth had made Gillian behave like that? he wondered.

Gillian reached her room, locked the door and flung herself down on her bed. She hadn't been able to bear it—the crowd of friends, the gentle hints that she had missed her chance of a lifetime: 'Peter certainly seemed to like you at first,' the knowledge that she would never see him again, that there was nothing but sorrow ahead of her. It had all been too much, the tears embarrassingly near, her mother's eyes too shrewd to face, even Peter had seemed to stare at her more than usual as if something about her puzzled him.

How could she bear it . . . how could she?! She clung to the pillow, digging her fingers deep into it, trying to stop the sobs. Why, oh why, had love to be so painful . . . ?

There was a gentle knock on the door and her mother's voice. 'Are you all right, darling?'

'Yes, Mum. I've taken some aspirin.'

'All right, darling. Have a good night.'

Gillian heard the stairs creak as her mother descended them. *Have a good night*. Could anything be funnier?

She heard the visitors go much later, recognized voices as they chatted on the porch. Even heard Peter's . . . and that made it worse. He was leaving soon after dawn the next morning, he had said, as it was a long drive.

Suddenly something made her jump out of bed and go to the window. It was not late, the sun still bright though falling. Yes, there was Peter . . . walking down the drive, pausing at the gate for a last look back.

Gillian hid behind the curtain. Had he seen her? She hoped not for it would be so terribly embarrassing for him. As Lucille had said . . .

She opened the drawer of her dressing-table, fumbled around under a pile of hankies and pulled out a letter. She straightened it and read it for the hundredth or so time.

'How can I thank you, Gillian, for the way you have helped us. Peter has told me what you have done. Two more weeks and Peter will be back in his beloved London, doing the work he loves, being near me. As he has so often written, the time has dragged and he longs to be back with me again. He owes you so much but he is shy and easily embarrassed and asked me to tell you. We'll send you an invitation to the wedding. You simply must come.'

Gillian gave a little moan and dived for the bed, burrowing her head in the pillow as the tears came.

She was awake early, hiding behind her curtain, watching the road. She saw Peter's car come down the hill and then he was gone. Gone for ever.

Now she must find a way to forget him—to make herself believe he never even existed.

It was easier said than done, she realized at breakfast. Her father was reading the local paper when she joined them.

'Pity about last night, Gillian. Bit of a slap in the face for Peter, wasn't it? Surely your headache wasn't as bad as that?' he said, quite gruffly.

'I'm sorry . . .' she said, not looking at him.

'Gillian, what is the matter with you?' he said, sounding exasperated. 'You've changed so much.'

And suddenly she knew what she must do. She looked up.

'I think I've got itchy feet, Dad. I'm tired of this backwater, I want to see the world . . .'

She saw the shocked surprise on her parents' face, but went on, thinking as she spoke, realizing that this could be the solution.

'I could sell the Riding School and the horses and with the money go abroad—United States, Canada or Australia, I haven't decided, and get a job. I'd like to see the world and . . .'

'But Gillian darling, you've been so happy here.'

'*Been* is right, Mum. I have been happy here but there comes a time when you want a change, to meet more people.'

'Well darling, of course if that's what you want . . .' Gwen Yelton sounded bewildered. 'It's so unlike you.'

'I'm not sure that it isn't a good idea.' Philip Yelton said slowly. 'We'll talk about it tonight, Gillian, for I may be able to find a buyer for the school . . .' He stood up, glancing at his watch. 'We'd better get going, Gwen. By the way, I don't know how true it is but there's a rumour that the Council are going to do something about danger signs for the headland. Apparently Peter not only said some strong things to the local paper but actually got in touch with the Council and the MP. I'll be in the car, Gwen.'

Gwen Yelton stood up slowly. She looked and felt stunned. 'It's Dirk, isn't it, Gillian darling? Dirk . . . I never did trust that ghastly-looking creature.'

'Please Mum . . . you know how I feel . . .' Gillian gulped down her coffee.

At the door, Gwen turned, 'Why you had to fall for that kind of person I can't think. Why couldn't it have been someone nice like Peter?'

Gillian watched the door shut and closed her eyes with a deep sigh. If they only knew!

It was an endless terrible day, a cold day despite the sunshine. What would happen to the dogs, she wondered. And would the new owners of the horses be kind to them? Where was she to go? Canada sounded cold though everyone said it wasn't, the United States sounded thrilling but everyone said the cost of living was terribly high and she might find it hard to get a job, Australia had sunny beaches but it was twelve thousand miles away and . . .

And, of course, the truth was that she had no desire to go away. She loved Pendennis and their little cove, she loved England, she was happy here . . . or she had been. If only Peter had never come down, if only . . . if only . . .

That night her father discussed the matter with her.

'You don't want to rush into it, Gillian. There's no hurry . . .' he said, as they had coffee after dinner.

She twisted her fingers together, careful not to look at him. 'Oh, there is. There is, Dad. I just can't wait to get away . . .'

Away to a new country, with new faces, new problems so that she could stop thinking about Peter. She glanced at the clock—was he in London already? Lucille in his arms? He hadn't said if he was going to stop on the way back as he had coming down, calling in on some old friends. If only she knew where he was so that she could think about him . . . and yet if she did know, perhaps it would make it all worse.

'Something's upset you, Gillian. I wish you'd tell us,' her mother leaned forward, her face anxious. 'You love Dirk?'

'Mum, please, I'd rather not discuss it. I am not going to marry Dirk, obviously, or else I wouldn't want to go abroad. Look, I've lived here all my life . . . or most of it. Is it so very surprising that I want to see the world?'

'Decided where to go?' her father asked.

'Not . . . not yet.'

'Well, I'll pass the word round that you might be interested in selling the Riding School and we'll see what bites we get. Meanwhile you'd better get some brochures and information about the countries you fancy.'

'Really Philip, do you have to encourage her?' Gwen Yelton said crossly.

Her husband smiled at her. 'It's Gillian's life, my dear. The least we can do is to help her.'

Next day, Gillian went into Cudjack and to the only Travelling Agency, returning home with a pile of brochures. It was a wet day and matched her feelings. She lit a fire in the lounge and lay on the rug in front of it, going through the gaily coloured brochures, the dogs by her side.

Australia had some lovely beaches, some beautiful green spaces, some thrilling looking mountains. Canada had the Rockies and all that crisp clean look. America was exciting . . .

Nanny brought in lunch on a tray and looked as if she had been crying.

'D'you have to go, Gillian?' she asked. 'I don't know what we'll do without you.'

Gillian was tempted to tell her the truth— but Nanny might consider it her *duty* to pass the news on to Gillian's parents.

'I'm not going for ever, Nanny.'

'That's what they all say but they never come back. I only hope you know what you're doing, Gillian. I've no time for foreign places myself. England is where I was born and where I'll die—no better place in all the world, that's what I say, and what you can find wrong with it, I can't think . . .'

She slammed the door as she left the room and Gillian pulled a rueful face as she ate her lunch. She sighed, a deep heavy sigh. If only . . .

After lunch she went out to the stables. Old Brummel was in a bad mood.

'Never thought you'd do this, Miss Gillian, selling up—and after all the care we've given them,' he grumbled.

'I'll only sell them to good people,' she promised.

Her work in the stables made her feel even more unhappy. This was her life—her way of living. How could she give it all up and go thousands of miles away, all alone, to build a new life.

201

And how, she asked herself sternly, could she bear to stay here where the memories of Peter were so painful . . .'

She stood still in the rain, startled, frightened for a moment for she thought she had seen a ghost.

But it *was* Peter.

He came walking down the driveway towards her.

'Peter . . .' Her voice trembled and she drew a deep breath, as she tried to get control of herself. 'How on earth did you get here.'

'I flew down. Hadn't we better go in? You're getting very wet.'

Nanny came fussing. 'Better go up and wash your face, Miss Gillian, and change your clothes. You're wet right through to your skin. How you exist, I don't know, doing such stupid things. A nice cup of tea, Dr. Richardson? There is a fire lit.'

'Thank you, Nanny, it's just what the doctor wants.'

They shared a laugh as Gillian hurried upstairs. She was trembling so much it took what seemed like ages to wash and change into jeans and a shirt. Then she stared in the mirror and pulled them off, changing into a pink frock. She stared at herself—there was little improvement. In any case, what did it matter what she looked like. To Peter, she was just *a sweet child*.

'Miss Gillian, what's coming over you . . .'

Dr. Richardson's waiting . . .' Nanny called up the stairs crossly. 'Really, Dr. Richardson, she's not the girl she used to be. She's changed so much . . .'

Gillian almost fell down the stairs to stop Nanny from talking. Goodness knew what she'd say next.

Nanny had shooed the dogs ouside, grumbling at their muddy paws. 'They'll only make poor Dr. Richardson all muddy,' she had said when Gillian protested.

There was a strange silence in the room when Gillian closed the door. Peter had poured out the tea. He indicated the couch for her to sit down and handed her her cup and saucer. He stood in front of the fire, drinking his tea and looking down at her.

'Did Lucille ever come and see you?' he asked abruptly.

She went bright red and hesitated.

'I know she did. She told me,' he went on.

Gillian relaxed. 'Then that's all right. She told me not to tell you because you got embarrassed. She said . . . she said you were upset because the local gossips said I was . . . I was chasing you . . .'

He put his cup and saucer down but went back to the fire, standing very straight, hands clasped as he looked at her.

'I see. Were you?'

The colour blazed in Gillian's cheeks. 'I . . . I didn't mean to . . .'

'I know you didn't. And I'm equally sure the local gossips were not saying you did. I gather Lucille asked you to leave me alone because I was hers?' His voice was cold.

Gillian swallowed. 'Yes. She said you were engaged to be married but that there were complications. That you were longing to go back to . . .'

'My beloved London. She wrote you a letter?'

Gillian nodded. 'She said you wanted her to thank me. That you were longing to get back to your beloved London and her.'

'I see. I thought at the time that you knew about the two weeks left to me—before I knew. I met Mrs. Oswald and she knew I was going.'

'Yes, I told her. I thought . . . well, I didn't think it was a secret or anything.'

'Naturally. I wondered at the time how she and you knew—then you talked of my beloved London, I guessed Lucille had written to you.'

'But hadn't she told you?'

He gave a strange sort of smile. 'No. By the way, I understand Lucille asked you to do her a little favour. Or rather, do *us* a favour.' He watched the colour in Gillian's cheeks. 'Was that why you pretended you were having an affair with Dirk? Was that all lies?'

Gillian's head drooped. 'Yes.' She was afraid to look at him in case he recognized the truth.

'I see . . .' Peter began to pace up and down the room restlessly. 'You were never in love with Dirk?'

'No . . . no, never. Peter—I promised not to tell anyone so you mustn't but . . . but Dirk is only seventeen. He's still at school, it's a long story.'

Peter smiled, for the first time. 'I thought he was young. So, for once, I was right.'

He paused, looking down at Gillian. He seemed very tall, so terribly attractive.

'Gillian, I have something to tell you.'

She caught her breath, felt her body tense as she clenched her hands. He was going to tell her that he and Lucille were to be married. He would invite her to the wedding. How could she go? But how could she refuse without him guessing the truth?

'Gillian, remember we talked about our ambitions? Mine was solely to do with my work? Well, I've changed my mind. My ambition now is to be married . . .'

She closed her eyes and held her breath. Here it came . . .

'And have four children,' he added.

Startled, she opened her eyes and stared at him.

'I was thinking, Gillian,' he went on, 'that as we both have the same ambition, it might be a good idea if we married one another.'

She couldn't speak for a moment. 'If we . . .'

He moved swiftly, kneeling down by her

side, his arms round her, his mouth on hers. 'Darling . . .' he whispered in her ear as his mouth moved gently over her face. 'I've never been in love before so I'm not sure what to say.'

'Peter . . .' she cried out joyfully, her arms tight round his neck. 'Peter darling . . . I can't believe it . . . It can't be true.'

He held her very close 'But it is true. I don't know when I first began to love you but I thought you loved Dirk.'

She moved slightly away so that she could gaze into his face. 'How did you find out?'

'Last night Lucille took me out to dinner. I had already guessed she'd been trying to mess things up so I bluffed her into thinking you'd told me. She lost her temper and I got the whole truth. I was afraid she might write to you and you believe her so I had to get down here fast. That's why I got a 'plane down. Would you have believed her?'

Gently, almost fearfully as if it could not possibly be true, Gillian stroked his cheek. 'I'm afraid so for I really thought you loved her. She's so very beautiful.'

'You're far more lovely,' he told her and she knew he meant it. 'I never have liked Lucille. I hate being chased.'

Her cheeks glowed. 'You didn't think I chased you when you first came?'

'Certainly not. I was simply a lame duck you were helping.'